WHICH WAY THE CAST JUMPS

CREATURES OF THE MIDWEST PREQUEL

AVA SILVERS

BLURB

A witch who has lost magic, turned vampire, wants to find who cursed the vampires.

Without her magic Opal isn't as powerful as she needs to be to save those she cares about. If she's not careful the others may find out about her secret and then she would lose her position in the cast.

But that's not the biggest problem she's facing, there's something odd with the vampire blood, it's tainted, some died and some didn't during the purge. This has something to do with the vampires having witch friends... why would someone put a curse on the vampires?

The path she is on is pulling her into dark magic where the only way out of the entrapment would be death.

Opal, with the help of a good witch Vivien, and vampire Cyrus, is determined to find out why there is a connection between vampires and witches and to find out who cursed the vampires to reverse the spell.

Unaware when she arrived at the sleepy seemingly innocent small town, Shadow Hollow, that her blood could open the portal to hell, and nothing that had unfolded was by chance. Will she pay with her life?

For the witches, keepers of magic and seekers of truth,
Love
Ava Silvers

WHICH WAY THE CAST JUMPS

CHAPTER
ONE

I f my big sister knew I'd spent the last five years lying, cheating, and stealing my way across the world, she'd skin my hide, bury me beneath Aunt Mags' favorite willow tree, and then set the whole lot on fire.

Gods forbid, she found out I wasn't even human anymore. She'd probably find a way to erase my existence entirely.

At least when I paused my jetsetting long enough to stay in Shadow Hollow, rubbing elbows with the coven, I could pretend to be the Goode witch my mama raised us to be.

Christina Steele's deep, throaty voice filled the room with the final incantation. I lifted my arms to the ceiling and closed my eyes, wishing with a kind of bone-deep longing that I could actually feel the magic swirling around me. The combined power of the coven used to feel like a blanket wrapped around my soul on a dark winter's night. I could only imagine how heady the power felt right now with little more than a week until Samhain, when the veil between this world and the next grew thinnest.

"We beg blessings of fruit from the Earth Mother's womb," Christina intoned, her pretty, heart-shaped face turned to the ceiling. She was a tall, thin, athletic woman with deep caramel skin and stick-straight black hair, and on top of the beauty, she had the power to boot. A Steele witch. An air witch. If I imagined real hard, I could sense the wind whipping around her.

I really fucking missed magic.

"For each child and each crone, may rich harvests bloom," Christina finished. "So mote it be!"

"So mote it be!" I parroted, my voice in concert with the twenty or so women packed into Christina's basement.

The Crazy Woman Coven left little to chance - not with Gayle Greene's infamous "protection" all but faded. Every month during farming season, we performed this spell to ensure all the crops in the area remained plentiful. Shadow Hollow might not have been rural, per se, but much of our surrounding lands depended on farming, both crops and livestock ranches. They were a driving force in our community, and whether the farmers believed in magic or not, they appreciated whatever help we could give them.

Our community. So weird to say that. I hadn't

meant to put down roots, but here I was. I'd been here three months now. My longest run in a single place, and a lifetime in my world of racing from town to city before grass could grow beneath my feet.

As a group, we tramped upstairs to Christina's modern stainless steel kitchen. She'd left the verandah doors open on her paradise of a backyard, and outside the moon was nothing but a sliver of silvery light. It would be full four days after Halloween, which only added to the feeling of growing occult power as we raced towards the high holiday that represented the thinning of the veil between the living and the dead.

We filled our plates and glasses, then a comfortable chatter settled over the room. I found an empty seat and dug into the spiced tomato and egg casserole Keya Leghari had brought, wishing I'd spooned extra onto my plate. While I ate, I watched Christina working the room as she always did when she hosted the coven at her house. She looked elegant and easy, her long hair swishing around her slender shoulders, and her smile lighting up the room as she floated from person to person, greeting, touching, always smiling.

Maybe one day, I'd have a place of my own where I could play hostess, too. Imagine—me growing *those* kinds of roots.

"Willow Goode. I wish my ass looked as good in jumpers as yours does." Alice Autumn hopped up onto a stool next to me at the kitchen island. She appraised me with dark brown eyes that always seemed to see more than what lay on the surface. Probably did, too. "You look tired."

"I'm not sleeping well," I agreed, reaching for the pitcher of sangria to top off my already half-empty glass. I poured liberally, then turned the spout over Alice's glass, too, because a good southern girl never drinks alone. "Nightmares."

Alice plucked a sweet roll off the tray in front of us. "About anything in particular?"

"My mom. It was this time of year when…" I trailed off. I didn't *have* to say the words. Alice already knew my mother was dead.

"Oh, man, Willow. I'm so sorry." Alice wrapped a wiry arm around my shoulders and tugged me into a tight half-hug, both of us hanging awkwardly off our stools to reach each other. "Hey, you should come into the shop and get a reading. Maybe it would help give you a little insight into coping."

Alice owned Mystique, a little occult shop down on the town square that did a brisk business. Back before I'd lost my powers, I'd been a big chunk of that brisk business, and I still made a point to buy things every now and then, just to support her. She was one of the few people who knew what had happened.

Why I had no more magic.

"I'd like that," I agreed. "Any day in particular?"

We chatted a while longer, and eventually, women began to trickle out in twos and threes. Around nine-thirty, Alice excused herself for a date, and Keya stopped by my seat to ask me what I thought of her curry casserole. I didn't have enough adjectives to describe my level of enchantment, but I was pretty sure I got my point across with, "Will you marry me?" Unfortunately, neither of us actually swung that way, and Keya had been married almost thirty years, but the point still stood.

Finally, it was just me and Christina, and we settled into our usual clean-up routine. I busied myself folding the nice, white wooden lawn chairs so I didn't have to look her in the eye as I asked, "Do you think they suspect anything?"

I asked every time. Every coven meeting. The rest of the group didn't know that my powers no longer existed, and I wanted to keep it that way. When a Goode witch had joined the coven, it had empowered the group into an excited frenzy. *A Goode witch and a Steele witch! Shadow Hollow might be protected yet...*

When I was no longer a Goode witch - at least, not in power, if still in name - I hadn't wanted to break their hearts by telling them. I'd left for a few months. Traveled the world, bounced in and out of Shadow Hollow like a ping pong ball on a long way down. Kept myself sparse so that I wouldn't have to tell the coven that I wasn't the witch prophesied to protect Shadow Hollow.

"Oh, come on, Will. Stop acting like you made a deal with the devil." Christina dumped the dredges of a sandwich tray into the trash can then tossed a twinkling gaze at me. She had eyes so dark not even the depths of the universe could rival them.

"Corwin's not the devil," I said with a laugh. "And you know it."

"If anyone's the devil, it's my fiancé." Christina rolled her eyes and turned around to gather a handful of red Solo cups from the patio table.

"Yeah, how is wedding planning treating you, anyway?"

Christina tossed the stack of cups at the trash can. "I haven't started yet. Don't ask."

"If you need to run away, you can always come stay with me and Sarah. There's a couch. It's not very comfortable, and you'll have to sleep with Sarah's cats, but there's not much chance your straight-laced, 'demon' of a fiance would show up on that doorstep."

I'd only met Neil Capstan once, and I hadn't been a fan. His dad and Christina's dad were colleagues, and their upcoming-but-not-yet-planned nuptials had been a kind of modern-day arrangement. I didn't ask questions, because it wasn't my damn business, but something unsettled me about Neil. Back before I'd lost my powers, my fire magic had gone haywire around him.

At least now, I wouldn't set anything on fire if he showed up after a coven meeting.

I could always find a silver lining.

Even if it was covered in blood.

Iᴛ ᴡᴀs ᴊᴜsᴛ shy of eleven when I parked my little rented Veloster outside Sarah Woode's cottage. Usually, I'd be in the car with Sarah, and we both would have stayed behind to help clean up, but she'd backed out of the meeting tonight, saying she didn't feel well. Sarah constituted the closest thing I had to a best friend, so she'd been on my mind most of the evening, and I was itching to get inside and check on her.

Corwin's sleek black Audi crouched in the driveway, cutting a stark contrast to Sarah's vintage Volkswagen beetle and old world cottage. Gray stucco walls, weathered by time and peaked in multiple gables with black, witch's hat roofs, plus a front lawn that spilled over with flowers and bushes, perfectly manicured by Sarah's green thumb. Most of the windows were dark, except for the large picture window on the side of the house that, during the day, let sunshine fill the kitchen. Tonight, amber light slanted across the grass, turning the shadows in the side yard darker than usual.

I locked the car doors, even though we were in the middle of nowhere outside city limits, because if I didn't, Aunt Mags would haunt me, then let myself in the front door. "I'm home! Sarah?"

"We're in here, Will," Sarah called, her voice sounding pale and tired.

Concern at her tone made the skin between my

brows knot painfully, and I dropped my car keys on the hall table before I went to join them.

They sat at the big wooden table while a small, merry fire crackled in the grate. A tea kettle still steamed on the stove, and one of Sarah's cream-colored Persians lounged in the middle of the room, purring loud enough to wake the dead. I stooped to pet his belly - Castor, distinguishable from his brother, Pollux, by the single dark spot on his chest - then continued to the table.

Corwin and Sarah faced each other across the table, mugs in front of them, though the liquid inside both was barely touched. Corwin's long blonde hair was pulled back in a messy bun, and there were dark circles beneath his eyes. But if Corwin looked tired, Sarah looked worse. Her auburn hair hung lank around her thin face, and her oversized sweatshirt swallowed her skinny shoulders. Her long bare legs were twisted into a pretzel beneath her, and I caught a glimpse of Pollux curled up in her lap, his blue eyes reflecting the firelight.

"Did someone die?" I greeted them, too wigged out by the dire atmosphere in the room to realize that wasn't really a PC way to start a conversation.

"Not yet," Corwin said darkly, and Sarah shot him a glare that could have peeled the paint off the walls.

Sighing, Sarah folded her arms around Pollux and leaned into the edge of the table as if it were the only thing holding her upright. "We need to talk."

I sank into a chair between them, giving Corwin my best *What-the-hell-is-happening?* look. He just shrugged.

"Are you breaking up with me?" I joked, though the little skip in my chest that was my sluggish, undead heartbeat told me the thought really terrified me.

I'd known them both for ages, even long before they'd started dating. When they started to get serious about a year ago, I thought this might happen one day. That Corwin would move completely in with Sarah, and they'd give me the boot. Maybe he'd let me live in the big Queen Anne he owned in a historic neighborhood across town.

"Don't be silly," Sarah said, flashing a wan smile. "I'd never do that. Our lives are better because you're in them."

"Ditto," I replied. "But by the dire atmosphere, I somehow don't think this meeting was meant for undying declarations of friendship and love."

"No, actually, it's not." Sarah took a shaky breath, then visibly steeled herself. Tears pooled in her blue eyes, and Corwin's face looked like stone as she said, "Remember your diagnosis?"

My heart stopped its fake beating and crash landed in my stomach. "How could I ever forget being told I had an expiration date earlier than a gallon of milk?"

Sarah laughed, even though it wasn't the first time

I'd made that particular joke. "Well, it's not ALS, like you, but it's something just as deadly."

I swallowed hard. "Cancer?"

"Brain tumor," she corrected, her voice clogged with unshed tears. Corwin remained mute, raw anger mixed with terror on his face. "Growing fast and completely inoperable. They said I'd break down once it began pressing on certain parts of my brain. I'll lose motor function, memory. I'll turn violent and angry. And there's nothing they can do. No treatment. No surgery."

I glanced at Corwin, but he gave no sign he noticed. "Well, it's fine, right? Corwin can just turn you like he did me. I mean, you'll lose your powers, and the blood cravings aren't ideal, but you'll be alive."

"Tell that to him." Sarah's chin jutted out as she gave her boyfriend a scathing look.

I'd known Corwin longer than Sarah, and I knew he hated being a vampire. It wasn't a life he'd asked for. He'd been a perfectly healthy man with a home and a family, and when his sire turned him, he'd been given no choice in the matter. But I also knew that when it came to Sarah Woode, Corwin melted like a chocolate bar on a hot Georgia sidewalk.

I leaned onto my elbows and addressed him. "This isn't the same as your situation, Corwin. I weighed my options and made my choice, and I'd much rather be alive than dead. Sarah's a big girl. She can make this decision, too. You aren't taking her free will from her like your sire did to you."

"It only makes sense," Sarah added. "If you two aren't going to grow old, I might as well join the club. Right?"

"Ask Willow if she has any regrets," Corwin said stiffly.

Sarah's red-rimmed gaze turned back to me.

"I miss my powers," I said with a shrug. "We didn't know when he turned me that I'd lose them. That part doesn't get any easier. You would *never* be able to perform any magic ever again. I didn't realize how much I actually depended on my abilities until they were gone."

She nodded. "But would you take it back?"

"Fuck no. I like being on this side of the grave, even if it's a weird kind of in-between place where I like my steaks rare."

Corwin made a low noise of dissent and hurtled from his chair with preternatural vampire speed. He went to the window to look out at the night, his hands laced behind his back. I knew this move—this was classic Corwin avoidance.

Sarah sighed again, and I wondered how many times they'd gone around and around this subject before now. "I've seen the struggle you've gone through. The... difficulties." She grimaced and wrapped her hands around her mug. "The lack of magic, the inability to perform the simplest spells. How gross it is to drink blood. I know what it means."

"Do you?" Corwin snapped, whirling on his heel. He moved with that eerie, vampire speed that my own undead sight registered in slow motion. But for Sarah, it would have looked like he was at the window one moment, and the next, he'd yanked her off the chair and wedged her against his body with a vicious snarl.

His fangs bared over her throat.

That was my cue to leave.

"I support your decision," I called over the sound of Corwin's growls. "But y'all gotta work out... this." I waved a hand at them. They looked like some All-American teen vampire movie, except neither of them were teens, and this wasn't a movie where Sarah would live in the end. She'd either die of a brain tumor, or become a vampire.

There was no other option.

Unfortunately, Corwin still needed some convincing, and that was *not* my job. He may have been my best friend, and the three of us had been thick as thieves for years, but their relationship had nothing to do with me. Quite frankly, I'd never been all that great at relationships to begin with, so I damn sure wasn't getting in the middle of this.

In my tiny bedroom at the back of the house, I

shed the yellow-and-white polka dotted jumper I'd worn to the coven meeting and waffled over putting on PJs or putting on regular clothes. If something happened, and Sarah needed a girls' night out, I wanted to be ready to be there for her. But on the other hand, I was also super ready to go to sleep. She'd woken me up at an ungodly hour this morning to go looking for mushrooms, like she did every single Saturday morning.

I was surprisingly not bothered over Sarah's situation. Maybe because I'd been there, done that, and I knew damn well that choosing an undead life meant she'd *have* a life. We had access to a kind of salvation, as bloody as it was, so, in my opinion, Sarah was just evolving beyond the tumor. No harm, no foul.

Corwin snapped something, his deep voice loud enough to penetrate my door but not loud enough for me to hear exactly what he said. I was trying *real* hard not to eavesdrop, but the tone of his voice left little room for interpretation. I cringed, thinking maybe Sarah needed a little moral support out there while I tugged a t-shirt over my head before reaching for a pair of green linen shorts.

I'd never been in love. Not the kind of love that Corwin and Sarah had—that forever kind, volatile and full of joy. One minute heaven, the next minute hell, and the whole damn journey a purgatory of good times, missteps, and lovemaking. I liked sex, and God knew I had no lack of willing partners from Shadow

Hollow to Timbuktu, but my interludes usually stopped at orgasm and steered well clear of affection.

I hadn't really felt that urgent, burning need for a steady man in my life. How boring would that be? I liked Willow Goode as she was nowadays, post-Turn with even more confidence than I'd had before I died and went Vampire. This ex-witch didn't need a man to complete her. Thanks to my older sister Hazel, I knew how to change the oil in my car, and I was perfectly capable of opening jars or smooshing bugs without a man to do those things for me. But if one day my so-called "Prince Charming" showed up at my door, I guess I wouldn't turn him away, either.

Somewhere deep in the giant, brown leather duffel bag I called a purse, my cell phone rang with a Destiny's Child song: "Bootylicious." It was a very specific ringtone for a very specific man who had an ass I wrote odes to in my head.

"Dante Bloode," I cooed into my phone. "To what do I owe this unexpected pleasure?"

Thick, molasses laughter rumbled over the phone line. "I'm coming to visit. Thought I'd warn you."

My libido did a little hop-skip, and I bit my lip, thinking about the last time he'd "come to visit." Oh, how he'd come. And I'd come. We'd both come for days.

Dante Bloode was front page, bad news. He came from a long line of dark witches with a hard-on for blood ritual, and his moral compass always seemed skewed a little south. But as long as it was skewed south on my body, he may as well keep up the bad work.

"More business for your dad?" I clarified.

"You know it."

"When?" I purred.

"Three days. Where you stayin' now?"

"With a friend."

"I'll get a room at the Old Circle Inn. Two beds?" There was a questioning note to his voice. The man was a sex god, but a sex god who preferred consent. I loved that about him. It was part of what kept me coming back for more.

"We'll only need one," I said, then hung up on him.

I grinned and placed my phone on the maplewood nightstand next to my twin bed. I couldn't wait to slide beneath the soft, white sheets at the Inn with a man hotter than Hades himself. Dante didn't come around often—he lived in California now, though he'd been born and raised in Georgia, like me, which contributed to his whole hot, Southern boy allure. You could take the girl out of Dixieland, but you couldn't make her stop turning to jelly at that deep, masculine twang.

The raised voices and urgent conversation had stalled in the kitchen while I'd been having my five second foreplay with Dante. I stepped into my slippers and then opened my bedroom door, craning an ear towards the rest of the house to try to make out any conversation.

Silence.

I heard a meow from somewhere close by and looked around the dark hallway to find one of the Persians sitting gracefully near Sarah's bedroom door.

"Are they done?" I asked him. I couldn't tell from this angle whether I was talking to Castor or Pollux.

He just stared at me enigmatically with his cool blue eyes.

"You're no help," I told the cat, then stepped outside and closed the door before I made my way to the kitchen to do damage control.

Corwin and Sarah were back in their seats at the table, staring each other down like they were a matador and a bull. I just didn't know who was which beast, though my money was on Sarah for the matador.

"Well, you haven't killed each other. That's good," I quipped, bypassing the table for the kettle on the stove. The water had grown a little lukewarm in the time since I got home, but I poured it over a chamomile mint tea bag, anyway.

"Not for lack of trying," Sarah snapped.

I brushed off her attitude, since I knew it wasn't aimed towards me, and leaned against the counter while my tea steeped. "Have we reached a decision?"

"Being a vampire is unpleasant," Corwin began.

"And dying is fun and games?" Sarah shot back.

I carried my full mug to the table, where they both glowered at each other so hotly I was afraid they'd set the house on fire. "I'm with Sarah on this one," I said as I slipped into a chair between them. "Dying for real isn't the preferable option. Dying to be undead is much better."

"Being a vampire isn't glamorous," Corwin said. "I've done my best to shield you from the... unpleasant aspects of my existen—"

"I haven't," I cut in.

He glared at me.

Shrugging, I went on. "Sarah's well aware of the 'unpleasant aspects.' She's helped me through a lot of things when I didn't feel comfortable bothering you. Quit treating her with kid gloves."

He bared his teeth at me, the coward. We both knew he loved Sarah Woode too much to deny her anything. Even if it broke his heart, he'd save her life if it meant turning her into the very thing he hated.

"Sarah..." He breathed her name, his face softening. "Are you sure? There's no going back once we do this."

The dejected look on his long, thin face tossed a wave of emotion over me. I wasn't used to Corwin being anything but stalwart. This despondent surrender was out of character for him, and it made the hairs on the back of my neck rise and tingle.

"You don't know what you're asking of me," he went on, his chocolate brown gaze dropping to his hands where they were twisted together on the table-top. "I love you more than life, so if this is what you truly wish, I'll make it so."

"It's what I truly wish," Sarah parroted, a note of steel in her voice.

Sarah put off this image that she was small, sweet, soft-spoken, and absolutely at the beck and call of anyone who needed her. Only Corwin and I knew the *real* Sarah—the fact that she had a backbone made of titanium and a mind sharp as a whip. If she'd made up her mind, she'd made up her mind. The only thing holding her back at this point was that she wanted Corwin to be her sire—not me. It formed an inescapable bond, an important bond, so of course she wanted him to be the one to do it.

"It's painful," Corwin replied. "It's not pleasant."

Sarah's chin tipped towards the ceiling. "I know."

Corwin swallowed visibly. "When do you want to do it?"

"No time like the present," Sarah said, glancing at me. "If you're both ready to hold my hand through the transition."

"You'll be secluded enough here, I suppose," Corwin said gruffly, then he glanced at me. "I'll stay tonight, if that's alright with Willow."

"Not even a question," I replied. "It's Sarah's house, not mine."

"Can we... have a minute?" Corwin asked me.

"Of course. I'll clean up a room in the cellar. You'll

want a comfortable bed and plenty of darkness for the first few hours," I said, giving my best friend an encouraging smile.

I left the two of them with their heads together, murmuring softly, and passed down the narrow wooden staircase that led beneath the cottage. I imagined they were talking about the plans they had made, the things they'd hoped would still come to pass. Maybe mourning the loss of her mortality and any hope Sarah might have had of bearing a child.

The cottage would have been a nice place to raise a family, I thought as I stepped off the bottom step and into the cellar. Half the underground level had been finished with drywall and tile floors forming two small bedrooms and a half-bath, while the other half of the cellar was one large, open space where Sarah stored her root vegetables and drying herbs. I could imagine the kids in these bedrooms, fighting over the small bathroom, arguing loudly over who got to use it first.

Not that we even knew if it was possible for Sarah and Corwin to conceive. For all intents and purposes, Corwin—and I—were dead. Like...*dead* dead. Like he didn't have any living sperm to impregnate a human woman. Of course, that didn't keep them from adoption or in-vitro, which would have been a lot easier to do if Sarah were human.

Turning vampire would change a very, very big portion of her life.

I made sure the smallest bedroom, the one with no

window, had clean sheets on the small trundle bed, then rifled around in the ancient, groaning refrigerator in the main room for a fresh bag of blood from the blood bank. She'd be hungry as hell when she woke up, so it'd be best if a lukewarm bag of blood awaited her.

Even taking my time, I was done too soon. I didn't want to cut short their little tete-a-tete, but I hadn't exactly brought any form of entertainment down with me. So I headed back upstairs.

Despite my worry they wouldn't be done saying what needed to be said, they were both silent when I stepped off the stairs into the kitchen.

"Any last spells you want to cast?" I asked Sarah, going for levity.

She perked up. "Actually, yes. I've been working on a way to make your daywalker charms permanent, and I just finished the incantation this week."

"Might as well add a third one," I suggested. "For yourself."

Sarah nodded. "Good call. Meet me in the ritual space in five."

She looked more like herself as she shoved her chair away from the table and leapt to her feet to go gather whatever she needed for the spell. Corwin, on the other hand, looked fit to murder me in my sleep.

He stalked toward me, his vampire speed less menacing since I could follow him easily. "You could have helped me talk her out of it."

"You want her to die?"

He growled at me like a rabid dog. "No, I want her to find another way!"

"You didn't fight me this hard when I made the decision. Hell, it was *your* idea originally," I pointed out. "Why is it different for Sarah?"

"Because I… I simply have a bad feeling. You might say intuition or gut instinct." He swallowed hard, and I didn't think I'd ever seen him look so fragile. "Something is wrong, and we shouldn't go through with this."

"Did you explain that to her?" I inclined my head to indicate Sarah, who was talking to herself in the other room as she searched out spell supplies.

"I did. She said I'm being too sensitive, and I'm projecting Jazmin onto her."

I sucked in a surprised breath. "Damn. That's harsh. Your sire was an evil demon hellbent on making your life hers. Sarah is a far cry from that monster."

Corwin shrugged helplessly. "I know. I'm powerless to stop this."

Resting a hand on his shoulder, I said softly, "Sarah made her choice. She wants to live. You can't fault her for that."

"No. I suppose not." He heaved a great big sigh, his shoulders slumping, then he brushed a hand over his tired face.

I offered him my hand. "Come on. Let's go help with her daywalker charm spell."

Sarah was already in the middle of her chalk circle when we entered the parlor, where she had a small podium set up as an altar. She'd placed a thick, silver-chained necklace on the podium next to an already lit black candle, and as we joined her, she motioned to it.

"Place your daywalker tokens next to mine."

Corwin fished his Persian coin from his pocket and placed it gently on the scarred wooden table top. I tugged off the chain around my neck and sat my own, custom-made charm next to his. Sarah had carved my half-dollar-sized coin with a beautiful, green tree of life on one side and a protection sigil on the other before blessing it the day before I was turned.

"Hold hands," Sarah told us, offering us each one of her own.

Her fingers were cool but stable in mine, while Corwin's usually steady hands had a bit of a tremor in them. If Sarah noticed, she didn't let on, so it was possible I could tell only because of my sensitive vampire abilities.

Sarah cleared her throat and closed her eyes. I imagined her fire power rising within her, heating the room, heating the space around her body. Just like I spent my entire time with the Crazy Woman Coven wishing I could feel Christina's air magic swirling around us, I wished now that I could feel Sarah's fire power. I wished I could become one with it, add my own fire to the mix and help her bolster the spell.

But I'd made my decision. I hoped she took her

time and cherished this moment, because soon, her powers would be gone forever.

She spoke.

"Our circle of three, bind us together
One for the daylight, One for the nether
One for the sisterhood, One for the heather
One for my heart, One for tomorrow
One for my life, One for my sorrow
One for eternity, One for the horror.
Together we're bound, together we strive
To honor and love each day we're alive."

As her voice trailed off, a frisson of energy rushed past me, and I could *just* barely sense it, as if it were more powerful than anything ever before. Then a dusting of rose petals began to fall around us, manifesting from mid-air and floating gently to the floor where they formed a perfect circle around us on the hardwood.

I stared at the rose petals in surprise. Sarah was a fire witch, not an earth witch. Now, granted, she was pretty good with a garden, and half our meals at home included vegetables and herbs she'd coaxed to life, but she wasn't an earth witch.

So how the living hell had she manifested rose petals from nothing?

"So mote it be," Sarah said, then put out a single bare foot and broke the ring of rose petals, breaking the circle.

I picked up my charm, but nothing felt different

about it. Then again, I couldn't sense the magic in the first place, so it was stupid to expect that to change now.

"Are you ready?" Sarah asked us, leaving her newly blessed daylight token necklace on the altar as she walked past us. "Let's do this."

We progressed down the hallway and took the stairs to the basement, my sluggish vampire heart thumping harder than the half-hearted attempts it usually gave. It didn't *need* to beat; more like, the memory of beating was so strong when my emotions were high, that it tried anyway.

I couldn't shake Corwin's certainty that something was wrong. He wasn't a mystical, woo-woo kind of a guy, so for him to put so much stock in his gut instinct, I couldn't help but think maybe he had good reason for it. Watching their backs ahead of me on the stairs, I thought about speaking up. Telling Sarah we should listen to Corwin's instinct. That maybe the time wasn't right or something.

But I didn't. Sarah had enough pushback from the man she loved. She didn't need it from her best friend, too. When I'd been turned a year and a half ago, everything went off without a hitch. We had no reason to believe tonight would be any different.

Corwin helped Sarah into the small bed, then hovered over her uncertainly. "Are you sure?"

"I have no doubts at all. I'm ready. I've made peace." Sarah reached out and entwined her fingers with his, making me feel like I was intruding on a private moment. "We'll have a new beginning together."

He nodded, though the uncertain look in his eye didn't fade. Sarah tugged him down for a long kiss that was just shy of indecent, considering the bestie was in the room, but then Corwin broke away and brushed back her mane of auburn hair, exposing her long, pale neck.

Their gazes met for another long moment, and then she ever-so-slightly tilted her head away from him, giving him more of her throat.

I saw the hunger when it hit his eyes. The blood-lust was all-consuming, especially for a vampire like Corwin who subsisted on bagged blood because he refused to drink straight from the source. When I was with him, I did the same, but when I was out in the world, doing my own thing, I found plenty of men willing to open a vein once I got my hands on them. I didn't have to kill to get my fix, and sinking my teeth into a man's skin while in bed with him was the height of pleasure for me. And them, too.

It occurred to me that Corwin had probably never drank Sarah's blood. He harbored so much disdain for being a vampire that he refused to do even basic vampire things. Coupled with their physical relationship, this would probably be an even *more* private moment that I shouldn't be privy to. But she wanted me here, so I stayed, a voyeur to an unspeakable act of love and violence.

As Corwin's teeth pierced her flesh, Sarah cried out. I remembered that moment, when his teeth tore into me. It burned like a brand, before he began to suck, and the motion turned languid and sexual, even between me and Corwin while we were just friends. Sarah's gasp turned to a moan, and her pink-tipped fingernails sank into his arm, drawing him closer. He crawled onto the bed, their bodies melding together, and I wanted to avert my eyes, but I couldn't. Corwin's bloodlust wafted through the air like a perfume, and my mouth watered. My body reacted to all the pheromones, both vampire and human. My own sharp teeth distended when he broke free from her skin and the sweet, coppery tang of Sarah's blood drifted towards me on the air.

With a swift slash of his bloodied teeth, Corwin opened his wrist, then pressed the wound to Sarah's lips. She had to drink to complete the process—quickly, before his blood coagulated, before she died from the blood loss. It was an intricate dance—one that I knew Corwin had only completed a handful of times. But, despite his earlier misgivings, his movements were sure, and he lay beside her, watching carefully as she imbibed his blood before he gently extracted her mouth and urged her to lay back on the pillows.

From here, Sarah would be out of it for a while as

the transition worked its way through her body - shutting down organs, slowing her heart, slowing her blood. By morning, she'd be a vampire.

Corwin climbed off the bed to join me, a crystalline tear tracing a path down his cheek in the light burning down from overhead. "Well. It's done."

I took his hand and squeezed. "You did the right thing. Tomorrow, all your worries will seem like a bad dream."

"Right."

We stood there for half a moment, watching Sarah sleep. She'd be a beautiful vampire - it would change just enough about her appearance to make her more stunning, more luminous, just like it did for me. Part of the magic of it, I guess. Makes a girl undeniably sexy to men so she'd have a veritable buffet to choose from.

"Come on. Let's leave her to percolate." I dropped Corwin's hand and turned for the door, just as Sarah's eyes flew open, and she retched.

She sat straight up in bed, her hands fluttering to her throat and her eyes going wider than seemed physically possible. She choked as if she couldn't breathe, and then, a moment later, viscous blood gushed out of her mouth, spraying the bed in a crimson flood.

"Sarah!" Corwin launched back across the small room, ignoring the blood as he took her in his arms.

But she made no move to indicate she heard him. Her eyes were unfocused, glazed, and she continued retching, blood spewing from her until there was nothing else to come out. Then she fell back against Corwin, her body seizing and her eyes rolling into the back of her head.

"What's happening?" I gasped, hovering at the edge of the bed, my slippers slick with blood.

"I—I don't know!" Corwin pried Sarah's mouth open and turned her on her side. "She's having a bad reaction—a seizure—I don't know!"

For several long, terrifying moments, Corwin held Sarah's writhing body to the mattress and kept her from choking on her own bloody vomit. Then she gave one last, horrible contortion, and went still.

Corwin breathed hard from the effort of holding her in place—not because he needed the oxygen, but because of habit. He let go of her arms, one hand sliding to her neck to test her pulse. "No. No. No."

He flung himself off the bed, hitting the floor on his ass and scrambling away as if she'd burned him. He slithered through the lake of blood, dragging it across the room on his clothes.

Swallowing back a wave of terror, I stepped forward and put two fingers to Sarah's bloody neck.

She had no pulse.

Not even the thready, half-dead tap of a vampire's heart.

Sarah hadn't turned; she was dead.

Human dead.

THREE

My hand fell away from Sarah's neck, and I stared down at her beautiful corpse in a kind of haze. What had gone wrong? Had Sarah's body rejected the vampire venom? Was that even a *thing*?

I turned away from her, my stomach twisting with nausea as I searched out Corwin. He'd scooted all the way across the room and sat with his back against the wall, streaks of blood arcing away from him on the floor. His gaze was leveled with a preternatural steadiness on Sarah's deathly-still body.

"I don't understand," I said. My voice seemed out of place in the hush. The cute little sub-basement bedroom had suddenly become a tomb.

Corwin didn't answer right away. He stared dead-eyed at Sarah's still form, blood coating his front, soaking his hands.

"Corwin?"

Finally, he turned his glassy eyes on me. "I don't know. I don't know how... This wasn't supposed to happen. She should have... turned."

His gaze slithered back to Sarah, and he fell silent again.

I didn't want to pressure him to talk about it or to face it, and really, my own mind was in a bit of a fog, too. My best friend was *dead*, when only moments before I'd been internally planning an undead makeover after some serious retail therapy for both of us.

Now, Sarah was just... gone. Like my mom.

Never coming back.

Something pushed me to her side—some niggling of...something. Not anything I could pinpoint or explain, but enough of a nudge that I didn't think I was walking alone as I crossed the room and looked down at her corpse.

I coaxed Sarah's dead weight into a less violent posi-tion, pressing her arms down to her sides, straightening her spine, tilting her face away from us so we didn't have to stare into her wide, bloodshot eyes. Then I pressed my hand to her chest, wishing I could feel her heartbeat, and bowed my head to say a little prayer to the gods.

That was when I felt it.

Magic.

After more than five years without my powers, the

sensation felt so foreign, I almost didn't recognize it. The feeling tingled over my fingertips like a warning, not a welcome, and I drew back, shocked.

"What is it?" Corwin asked.

"Magic," I murmured, shuddering.

I heard scrambling behind me, then squelching footsteps as Corwin joined me at the bedside. "Coven magic?"

"No. It's not..." I trailed off, rubbing my fingers together to ward away the tingles. "It's not good magic. It's a curse."

"Someone put a curse on Sarah?" Corwin roared, his eyes going crazed.

Before he could Hulk out and go burn down the whole of Shadow Hollow, I grabbed his arm, blood tacky beneath my fingertips. "Not a curse on Sarah. If it was a curse specifically against her, it would have taken us, too. The three of us are bound by her magic and that daywalker charm. Any magic that killed her would have reflected through our bond and killed us, too. It's something bigger."

Corwin stood so still beside me, it was as if he wasn't even there at all until he spoke again. "Can you find out what?"

Hesitantly, I reached out and touched Sarah's heart again. That oily, dark magic flowed beneath her skin, stronger than it had been before.

I'd wished for magic for the last year. I'd wished to

touch it, to feel it in my hands, to revel in the power on my skin.

But not like this.

"I can try," I said, my voice cracking. "Whatever it is, it's blood magic. Dark magic. And I don't know much about..." I trailed off, a ripple of shock straightening my spine. "Dante."

Corwin glanced down at me. "Beg pardon?"

"I have a friend who might be able to help us. He's coming to town Tuesday. In the meantime..." I reached out and smoothed Sarah's auburn hair. "What do we do now? How do we explain all this?" I gestured vaguely around the room, indicating the blood-covered bed and walls, the bite mark in Sarah's neck that hadn't had a chance to heal before she died, the fact that we had a dead body on our hands.

"We don't," Corwin said, voice hard. "I'll call Hooper, Weaver & Sons."

"The blood bank in Bozeman?" My brow wrinkled. "What can they do?"

"They aren't exactly a blood bank. They do..." He looked away from Sarah's body, closing his eyes against the pain that rested so plainly in his expression. "They do clean up, as well. They'll handle this, and come up with the necessary paperwork to indicate Sarah died of her disease."

I shuddered. "That's macabre."

"It's a necessary business in a world this dark," Corwin replied shortly. He'd traded his despair for his cast iron resolve, leaving behind a man that was more statue than vampire.

I'd always hated when he did this - when he looked so cold, so still, so inhuman. But I guess we all had our own means of coping.

He continued. "I'll get cleaned up and make the necessary phone calls. Will you sit with Sarah?"

Pain lanced through me, but I nodded. "Of course."

Then he headed back upstairs, still wearing Sarah's blood like a shirt, leaving me alone with my grief and my best friend's body growing as cold as my undead heart.

THE NEXT THREE days passed so quickly and painfully that I blocked most of it out by keeping a bottle of gin close and covering my real emotions with dark, inappropriate humor.

Hooper, Weaver & Sons were eerily great at what they did. A team of five young, nondescript men with nice muscles in their coveralls showed up before dawn, startling me from a light sleep in the chair beside Sarah. Two of them set about cleaning Sarah's body, while another duo unpacked bags and trunks full of industrial-strength cleaning supplies.

The fifth man took me by the arm and helped me upstairs to the kitchen, where he sat me at the table in front of my cold mug of tea from the night before, then set about making a fresh pot of coffee. With the way he served me coffee, cream, and sugar, you'd have thought he was making a pass at me. He was just attractive enough that I thought about asking him to join me in my bedroom, but somehow, through the haze of grief, I realized I was trying to heal my wounds with sex and refrained.

Before midday on Sunday, the house smelled of bleach, and the cellar had been momentarily transitioned into a morgue, where one of the clean up guys prepared Sarah for burial. He patched the bite wound in her neck so thoroughly, not even Sherlock Holmes could have discovered the truth. Then, bright and early Monday morning, she was carted to Shadow Hollow Funeral Home for the wake.

Hooper, Weaver & Sons handled all the arrangements. They even took care of the obituary, simultaneously announcing to the whole town that Sarah had been diagnosed with an inoperable brain tumor and then succumbed to her disease mere days later.

The five hour wake on Monday afternoon felt like it lasted days. Sarah had no immediate family—just a few cousins who drove in from southern parts of the state to pay their last respects. So Corwin and I handled the "family" portion of the funeral—standing beside the open coffin, greeting guests, making small talk, and thanking everybody on the gods' green earth for coming.

I hated every moment of it, because it reminded

me of my Aunt Mags' funeral. I'd been fourteen when Mags died, and my sister, Hazel, had just turned eighteen and recently graduated high school. The Goode family was large, and Mags had two surviving sisters, but the funeral had mainly fallen to Hazel and me, since Aspen and Maple were older and in ill health.

I'd loved Aunt Mags like a mother, but I'd hated the funeral. The pattern followed now with Sarah's wake and service, and I spent the vast majority of the day sneaking shots of gin in the bathroom and hiding the smell with peppermints.

By the end of the day, I never wanted to see another peppermint in my life.

Then we buried my best friend beneath a willow tree at Shadow Hollow's Resthaven Cemetery. After, Corwin and I sat on the grass beside a mound of fresh dirt, listening to the worms crawling with our preternatural vamp hearing. Silent. Grieving. Until we both lied down to rest right there beside Sarah's final resting place.

At first light Tuesday morning, Corwin drove me back to Sarah's cottage, pulling into the drive though he didn't cut the engine.

"You're not staying?" I asked, clutching my purse against my chest.

He shook his head, and a small muscle jerked in his jaw. The soft, warm porch lights gleamed off his dark eyes, making him look even more haunted than he already did. "No. I think I need to stay away for a while. I need...some time."

"Hiding isn't going to bring her back."

"No, but neither will surrounding myself with a house full of memories."

Touché. I leaned over and pressed a kiss to his cheek. He hadn't shaved in a few days, which wasn't normal Corwin behavior. Grief could manifest in so many different ways. Who was I to tell him what he could or couldn't do?

"Don't wallow too long," I told him. "The world is much better with you in it."

He didn't reply. I stood on the sidewalk and watched him drive away, hoping he wasn't going to do anything stupid like take his own life. I didn't think Corwin was that dramatic or Shakespearean about his lost love, but stranger things had happened.

The second problem with letting Corwin go hide away in his musty, antique mansion was that finding answers to Sarah's death would fall solely to me. Me, the girl who'd spent the past two days coping with her best friend's death sipping straight gin from an Evian water bottle.

Guess it was time to sober up and figure shit out.

I took a long shower so hot that it felt like it would slough the skin off my body. While I scrubbed my hair and shaved my legs, I ruminated over Sarah's mystical death.

I was ninety-five percent certain that magic had

killed Sarah, but I was one hundred percent certain I didn't have the powers or the means to test my theory. I'd spent most of Sunday remembering the slimy feel of the curse between my fingers, trying to place what it meant with my hazy memories of Aunt Mags' teachings.

Goode witches were one of the oldest, longest running matriarchal witch lines in history, a fact that was a point of pride in the Goode family nowadays. Our bloodline originated out of the Salem Witch Trials as a last bastion of defense for the *real* witches who barely escaped the Trials with their lives. Back then, women in Puritanical society were addressed as Goodwife, which was later shortened to Goody.

Goody Temperance Howell was a true, blooded witch with powers she hid well from everyone in town. When the hysteria began, she was the first to see the writing on the wall, and she began to smuggle the few true witches out of the Salem area, herding them down south to safe houses with other blood witches. She saved so many, the rest of the witches began to call her the Goode witch, and not long after she left Salem for points south, she dropped the name Howell and became Temperance Goode.

Temperance was legendary in our family. A powerful, even ruthless fire witch who put her life on the line to preserve the blooded witches—those born into magic. Never mind that she left the poor humans to suffer the hysteria by themselves. Nineteen of them went on to be executed for magic they didn't even *have* while Temperance was carting the real magical practitioners to safety.

I vaguely recalled Aunt Mags smoking a Pall Mall in front of the short, squat blackboard she used in our magical lessons. A wave of white smoke clouded her face as she told us Temperance was a hero, and how sometimes you had to sacrifice some to save the rest. I didn't exactly agree with the sentiment, but I couldn't deny I was proud to be a Goode witch.

The power of that name continued to protect me, even long after I couldn't protect myself.

But another memory was just out of reach from that same lesson. Pall Mall smoke. The trees creaking outside the open window, storms rolling into Marietta and dancing like raw, unburdened energy across my skin.

We'd talked about vampires that day.

Aunt Mags hated vampires. Treated them like second-rate citizens, scum of the earth, demon spawn that didn't deserve a place in our world. Bless her heart, she could be bigoted as hell, just like any other southern witch. I knew now, of course, that she was wrong in her estimations about their character.

She hadn't been wrong about their vulnerability to magic.

"That's it!" I shut off the water and wrung out my hair, grinning at the faucet.

That day in lessons, Aunt Mags taught us about a

witch who cursed vampires to walk in the night. Vampires weren't initially creatures of night. They lived and worked during the daytime just like witches. But something terrible happened, and this witch cast a vengeance curse, one that relegated vampires to darkness and made it so that any amount of sun would cause terrible burns.

In my bedroom, I dressed, trying to recall the details of the curse, but it had been ages ago, and I'd half not believed Mags when she said vampires were real. Which was funny enough, looking back now.

Of course, witches were clever beings, so daywalker tokens became a hot commodity not long after the curse took over.

But what if someone else had cast *another* curse on vampires? If one witch enacted her vengeance by keeping vampires from enjoying the sun, wouldn't it be possible that another witch might have come along with another ax to grind?

Maybe... by keeping them from siring new vampires.

But why had I survived the change and Sarah hadn't? Granted, I was turned a year and a half prior to Sarah's death. A lot could change in a year.

The doorbell chimed through the cottage, and I jumped, surprised by the sudden intrusion on my thoughts. I wasn't expecting company, though I guessed unexpected visitors in the wake of a loved one's death weren't out of the norm. I really didn't want to put up with yet one more person telling me how sorry they were while shoving a casserole dish into my hands. I hadn't yet finagled my generous breasts into a bra, so I just tossed a tank top on over my shorts and hurried to answer the door.

But it wasn't some Shadow Hollow local looking to pay their respects.

Dante Bloode leaned against the porch railing, looking for all the world like he belonged on the quaint porch of a twentieth-century cottage, when in reality, he wouldn't have been out of place in Hell. He wore his pitch black hair in a pompadour, slicked back with mousse, and the sides over his ears shaved to a close stubble. He usually dressed in black, preferring plain jeans and plain T-shirts over anything fancy, and today was no exception. A silver ring glinted in his eyebrow, and his vivid blue eyes immediately dropped to my chest.

The man always knew when I was braless.

"Not the greeting I expected, but definitely the greeting I deserve," he murmured, moving with a liquid grace as he came closer and snaked an arm around my waist to pull me against his body. One hand cupped my breast, and his thumb played across my nipple until it hardened against the fabric. Then he leaned down, closing the good foot of space between our heights to kiss me.

For a brief moment, I forgot Sarah. I forgot the possible curse, and my grief, and the fact I stood in a house that didn't belong to me. I forgot my own damn name as his tongue did things to my mouth that made me want to renounce all other men.

"Bedroom," he growled against my lips, and dipped his fingers beneath the waistband of my shorts.

Usually, I would have agreed and been naked in two-point-four seconds, but I needed to do something first. Something that would confirm the idea coming together in my head so strongly that I was able to unlock my lips from Dante's and shake my head.

"Soon," I promised him, giving a little wiggle against his very obvious desire pressing against his jeans. "But first—I need to kill a man."

FOUR

Dante's motorcycle roared between my legs as I clung to his waist on an off-ramp into Bozeman. We circled down to the main road, the bike tilting beneath us, and Dante squeezed the brakes, his abs flexing beneath my hand. I still couldn't believe I'd turned down sex in lieu of killing, especially sex with Dante who was my favorite flavor of fuck. But to Dante's credit, he was intrigued and seemed somewhat turned on by it. The dangers of screwing a dark witch—a little homicide before lunch was as normal as a blood curse by breakfast.

So I'd changed into my manhunting gear while I gave him a quick and dirty of the last three days. Then, wearing a dress so thin and so tight my Aunt Mags was probably rolling over in her pink satin-lined coffin, I climbed up behind Dante on his Harley, and we headed into the city.

I'd foregone a helmet, since a motorcycle crash could make mincemeat of me but *not* kill me, and my long ponytail whipped around my face as we came to a stop at the red light at the bottom of the ramp. I pulled my cell out of Dante's pocket as we waited, double and triple checking the address I'd been given.

I wasn't a monster. In my opinion—and Dante's, too—most people didn't deserve to die. Depraved human beings, however, were fair game, and there was no shortage of them to be found on the internet.

"Hank" had an ad on a deep web page that pandered to the darkest, most depraved fantasies a sociopath might have. *Hank* was looking for someone to eat. *Hank* was looking to make a Big Mac out of a person. Not because he was a vampire, but because he got off on the idea of murdering and eating another human being. A regular ol' modern day John Wayne Gacy, except, instead of little boys, Hank wanted a succulent young girl to quench his shades of pedophilia and cannibalism.

So I'd reached out through the web page's anonymous chat room to tell Hank how I was seventeen and my life sucked, and I didn't want to be alive anymore. But I had this *crazy* idea that if I was going to die, I wanted to see if someone eating me meant I could live on like all those cannibal tribes thought. I played up the woo-woo, crazy-pants aspect, thinking it would tease him into believing I was exactly the ribeye steak he desired. Then I sent him a picture of me in pigtails, hoping he'd bite, and he did.

Poor Hank. He was going to find out what the other end of the spectrum felt like—being the one who got eaten.

Bozeman was a large place with lots of hidey holes to disappear into, which meant I could do what needed doing without any undue attention. The GPS on my phone led us to an industrial district of old warehouses, some still in use but many so run-down and broken they'd likely never be useful again. Dante cut the engine, and we rolled into a spot a few blocks down from the chosen location, where he parked the bike and pocketed his keys.

Dante slid off the bike first, then turned to help me dismount. He got an eyeful of my lacy red thong beneath my dress, and his blue eyes darkened.

"I wish you'd worn something else," he said, voice a little breathless. "That dress makes me want to do bad things."

"And you will. *After* we off the pedophiliac canni-bal." But I pressed against him anyway with a kiss that promised more, thinking how strange my life had become that I'd uttered *that* phrase before having a man's hands up my skirt and his tongue in my mouth.

Not how I envisioned my life at twenty.

"You got the stake?" I asked when I finally pulled out of his grip and readjusted my dress.

"Right here." Dante whipped it out of his belt

beneath his shirt and twirled it through his long, elegant fingers like a vampire slayer.

"Good. If the turn *does* work, you kill him immediately."

Dante nodded. "And if it doesn't?"

"Then I was right, and someone's cursed vampires so we can't turn anyone new." I flashed a feral grin. "And he'll be dead anyways."

I walked towards the darkened warehouse, vividly aware of the blood pumping through Dante's veins as he disappeared into the shadows in the alley. He was going to find a back way in and hide until I finished the ritual, ready to leap to my rescue if Hank became a vampire.

The sun hadn't yet reached its mid-day point and was barely visible behind thick, dark clouds that promised rain. A brisk, fall wind whipped around my bare legs and I shivered, even though the cold never really bothered me, considering my body ran at a tepid room temperature rather than ninety-eight degrees. The general oogeyness likely came from what I was about to encounter, not from the October air.

The front door to the warehouse was unlocked, as Hank promised it would be. I scooted inside and guided the door shut so it wouldn't bang or otherwise alert Hank to my presence. I may have been playing a poor, tortured kid with a death wish, but I wasn't one. I wanted to get a bead on this guy before I let him lay eyes on me.

A faded logo on the wall announced Eclipse Industries with a half-torn eclipse and star cupping the words. Someone had spray painted unintelligible graffiti over half of the logo; it was just faded and distressed enough that normal eyes wouldn't have been able to make it out. I didn't know what Eclipse Industries made in this factory, but they sure as hell weren't making anything now. Birds were nesting over the old formica reception desk, and the floor across the lobby had collapsed in on itself, revealing a gaping scar straight down to the basement.

I followed a narrow white hallway away from the foyer and into the building, hoping the floors would hold me. Hank had told me to just "keep heading straight" and I'd find the interior warehouse, where he'd be waiting. Instead of following his instructions, I walked until I found a side hall and darted down it, silent in my sandals as I moved further into the building.

It didn't take too much effort to find the old work floor. Most of the administrative areas of the building led to the manufacturing areas, so I eventually found a thin door with a smudged window that looked out on an empty warehouse. Even through the dirty glass, I could make out stacks and stacks of metal shelves that had once held whatever goods Eclipse Industries had specialized in, and beyond, in the shadows, large industrial equipment covered in fine, white sheens of dust that made them look like giant ghosts.

The door squeaked ever so slightly, and I hesitated, my sluggish heart doing a little one-two-step before dying out again. But nothing moved, and somewhere further inside the warehouse, I heard a footstep shuffle, and then a man coughed.

Bingo.

Slipping onto the metal platform, I eased the door shut and then looked around for the stairs that would lead down onto the floor. Unfortunately, when I found them, they were nonexistent—just an opening in the railing where they used to be and a pile of rubble below.

Too bad being a vampire didn't come with the ability to become a bat. On the bright side, I was slightly more indestructible than your average human; a half-story leap to the ground would be no matter.

I hit the ground on both feet and then rolled, trying to absorb the shock of the fall and keep the sound from being loud enough to alert Hank. I rolled with the momentum until I was back on my feet, then hurried into the shadows behind the shelves.

Dante's blue eyes glittered from the end of the row ahead, and he pressed a finger to his lips before pointing to his right, through the shelving unit. He'd found Hank.

I peeked around the edge of the unit.

Hank was surprisingly normal. He had chestnut brown hair in a thick comb over, and he wore a pair of pressed blue jeans with a white polo shirt tucked into the waist. He sat in a metal folding chair, one arm resting on a card table and his fingers tapping rhythmically on the cushioned tabletop.

If I'd met Hank in a bar, I might have been stupid enough to go home with him. He was handsome, maybe a little bland, but some nights I got desperate for attention and I shot a little lower than my usual standard. If I'd been anything but a witch, and after that a vampire, he might even have eaten me without my permission.

How many people *had* he eaten without permission?

Guy had to go.

"Hank?" I called, pitching my voice so that it sounded as if I were coming from behind him. Another fun vampire prank that I just didn't get to use often enough.

He leapt to his feet like a frightened deer and whirled around, looking for me. By the time he turned back around, I was halfway across the empty concrete floor, already feeling better about my chances.

Easily tricked. Easily beaten.

As I walked towards him, my sandals slapping against the floor in the silent warehouse, his gaze raked over me with interest and something deeper— something hungry.

Ew. This coming from a girl who craved human blood. But I'd never eaten flesh and had no desire to start. I was a vampire, not a monster.

Hank giggled as I stopped in front of him, then licked his lips, his gaze dropping to my chest. "Nice dress."

"I thought... Well, I thought we could... you know. Before you do it." I pulled the hem of my dress up just shy of showing off anything important and made a lewd gesture to indicate my intentions. The leer that crossed his face made me want to vomit. "One last go before I'm dead, you know?"

Hank giggled again, this time a little more maniacally. "Oh. Yes, we can do that. I'd love to do that. Right now?"

He had a high, girlish voice with a bit of a lisp to it. Revulsion bubbled up inside me at the thought of what I'd have to pretend to do to get close enough to bite, but I shoved it away and stalked toward him in my best sex kitten walk. I could sense Dante in the shadows behind Hank, hiding behind the giant shelves that were weighed down by old metal parts, glass bins, and a decade of dust.

I walked right up to Hank, sliding my fingers up his shirt to hook a finger in his collar. Pressing my upper torso into his chest, I swallowed against the disgust trying to bubble up within me and said, "Aren't you going to touch me?"

Hank moved, his arm stilted as he lifted it up the front of my body. The backs of his fingers skimmed over my abdomen, then peaked over my tits, though they didn't stop there. I could taste Dante's fury on the air, and a surprising amount of possessiveness floated along with it.

I was surprised by that. Dante and I had always been casual. Hell, if there wasn't sex being offered in some way, shape, or form, we didn't ever communicate, not even via text. Did he... He couldn't have *feelings* for me. Bloode witches didn't have feelings.

I'd been so lost in my surprise, that I hadn't been paying attention to what Hank was up to. His hand curled around my neck, and I fought against my every instinct to fight back. Some guys got off on the whole alpha thing. They wanted control, wanted to be in charge, wanted to feel all manly or whatever. Lord their Big Bad Man Muscles over the little girl. So I let him tighten his grip, and I even threw in a little moan for good measure.

His grip tightened even more.

If I'd been a normal human, he would have cut off my windpipe, and I'd have been struggling to breathe. As it was, his fingers were digging painfully into my neck, bruising the sensitive skin and making all the tendons and important voice things inside scream mercy. But I didn't feel like I could complain or fight back. Not yet. Not until I could get the upper hand again and go in for my killing bite. The seduction had been my segue for that, and obviously, I'd failed miserably.

Suddenly, he pulled a gun from his waistband and put it to my head.

"I'm sorry," Hank said, his voice suddenly cool as a cucumber, deeper, almost as if he'd been taken over by someone else. "But I'm not sexually attracted to sluts."

Then he pulled the trigger.

Hank's bullet tore through my forehead with fiery rage, and I processed every single inch of the tiny metal piece's trajectory through my head. It exited out the back of my skull with another explosion of white hot agony, and my legs collapsed beneath me.

"Willow!" Dante's shout held a world of emotion, and I could hear his footsteps beating against the concrete floor as he raced for me.

I hit the ground on my side, momentarily stunned by the gunshot wound. My arms and legs didn't seem to be listening to my brain anymore, what with the trauma and all. But I could feel Dante's footsteps on the ground beneath my cheek, and I wished he'd run *away*.

Run away from the man with the gun.

"What the— Who the hell are you?" Hank seethed, then he fired his gun a second time.

No! I couldn't form the words. Couldn't move. Couldn't get to Dante to make sure he was all right. But it didn't matter, because I heard his body fall. With my senses heightened by vampire *and* by pain, Dante hitting the floor sounded like a third gun firing in my head.

"You brought someone else!" Hank shrieked. "That

wasn't in the plan, you stupid bitch. If I could kill you again, I would— Wait. You're still alive?"

Some of the haze had begun to clear away from my vision, and my brain was starting to pick up all the electric signals it had momentarily lost its grip on. I shifted my gaze away from the shadowy corner of the warehouse to find Hank standing over me, his gun hanging at his side and a look of pure disbelief on his face.

"You... you should be dead," he muttered, glancing down at his gun. "I shot you in the head. You're not even bleeding..."

I blinked once, twice, and some more of the haze cleared. Enough that I could sit up, even though my head still felt a little woozy.

Hank gasped and took a step back. "That's not possible."

Putting my palms flat to the floor, I dragged my knees beneath me, and then managed to get to my feet. My movements were painfully slow, as if the messages being sent from my brain to the rest of my body had been garbled by the bullet, but they were still being sent.

For a human man, it had to be the stuff of nightmares to see the woman he'd just shot getting to her feet.

When I'd finally straightened, I glared at Hank and twisted my hands into fists at my side. "You killed Dante."

Hank stumbled a step backwards, all hint of his previous control gone. "No. No, this is a dream. I'm dreaming."

I focused on putting one foot in front of the other and made my way towards him, never lowering my gaze, never letting the heat fall from my eyes. I could smell Dante's blood on the air. I'd tasted it before, and it was the sweetest thing that's ever been in my mouth, and now he was dead. Stolen from me.

Right as I realized I kinda actually maybe liked him. *Liked* liked him.

I snarled at Hank and put on a burst of vampire speed.

Hank backed away quicker, fear painting lines into his forehead. "Stay away from me! You're a demon! A monster!"

He lifted his gun to point it at me as if he'd just remembered he was carrying it, but I shot a hand out and batted it away from his fingers with little effort.

"I'm not a demon," I told him, this time wrapping *my* fingers around *his* neck. I dragged him to me with the full force of my vampire strength, and he began to blubber like a baby. "I'm a vampire. Don't you want to find out what it's like to be eaten?"

Then I sank my teeth into his neck.

Hank's blood tasted foul, like fruit that had been left to rot in the kitchen pantry until the flies set in. But I stayed the course, my fingers digging into his windpipe as he'd done to me while I drew his entire life's blood out the other side of his neck.

I kept drinking until I felt his heart slow and nearly stop. Then I released him, not really caring when he collapsed to the floor with a bone-jarring thump of his skull on the concrete.

He'd be dead in a few minutes. One way or another.

"Now, you piece of shit," I said, voice oddly calm despite the circumstances. You know, dead semi-boyfriend, bullet wound to the head, just another Tuesday. I knelt beside Hank and used my own teeth to tear into my wrist, then jammed the bloody wound against his lips. "Drink up."

Hank's mouth flapped uselessly at the air, and my blood stained his lips red. He wouldn't need to take much. Obviously, the more he could get before my sluggish blood dried up, the better. But just a few drops would do for the transition.

Once I was reasonably sure Hank had ingested enough, I left him lying prone on the concrete, blood still leaking from his sizable neck wound, and went to find Dante.

I didn't have to go far. He was sitting up a couple yards away, one hand pressed to his black T-shirt and his gaze on Hank's crumpled form.

"Have I ever told you you're scary as fuck?" Dante said, then hissed and made a face, closing his eyes as he readjusted his hand. "Motherfucker shot me."

"Motherfucker shot me, too," I quipped, dropping to my knees beside him. "I thought you were dead."

"Nah. I don't think he hit anything important." Dante's blue gaze eyed the hole in my head, but he refrained from any Swiss cheese comments.

"Hey," I said sternly. "Those rock hard abs are very important to me."

Dante grinned and leaned in to kiss me, just a quick peck but it felt almost... warm. Affectionate. "I'm glad you're not dead."

"Samesies." I picked up the hem of his t-shirt and cringed at the rapidly bleeding hole in his side. "We need to get you patched up. I know just the witch to do it."

Suddenly, from the other side of the room, the sound of retching filled the silent warehouse. I rotated on my knees to watch as Hank regurgitated the blood he'd taken from me, and then as his body seized and twisted. It was like watching Sarah die all over again, and the depth of my pain had no end as I remembered her sightless eyes and the fountain of blood.

When it was over, I tested the pulse in the cannibal's bloody neck.

Hank wouldn't be eating people ever again.

And I would never be able to get the taste of his rotten blood from my mouth.

CHAPTER

FIVE

I had a feeling the last thing Christina Steele expected to open her door to at noon on a Tuesday were two blood-covered people—one with a *literal* hole through her head—but not much could shake a Shadow Hollow's witch.

"Stars and stones," Christina cursed, stepping back to hold the door wider. "Get in before the neighbors see you."

With Dante's arm around my shoulders, I helped him hobble over the threshold and into Christina's spotlessly clean house, trying not to think of the bloody footprints he'd be leaving behind. The blood had slowed tremendously as I'd driven us back to Shadow Hollow on his motorcycle, but his entire lower half was soaked.

You never knew just how much blood existed in a human body until you began eating it for dinner.

"Here, bring him through here," Christina said urgently, opening a door near the downstairs bathroom to reveal a small spare bedroom.

"Not your nice floral bedclothes," Dante murmured, before collapsing onto those self-same floral bedclothes in all his bloody glory.

I picked up his feet and rolled him further onto the bed, then ripped his shirt away from his body to expose his wound. The bullet had entered his body to the far left, torn through muscle and the nonexistent layers of fat on his side before exiting out the back. It looked horrible, and the amount of blood staining his clothes made it seem like he had more outside his body than in, but he was right—the bullet hadn't hit anything major, or he'd be dead already.

Christina looked from Dante's bloody torso to the hole in my head. "What happened?"

"We got shot."

"I can see that," Christina snapped. "I mean, why on earth were you shot?"

"So... fun fact," I said. "It's physically impossible to turn a new vampire."

Christina leaned over and tugged Dante's t-shirt away from his back to eye the exit wound. "How do you mean?"

"Something's caused a barrier. Some kind of curse, I think. New vampires can no longer be made."

Christina straightened to look at me in surprise, still holding the bloody T-shirt edges in her manicured fingers. "Well, that explains the noticeable decline in the vampire population."

"You've noticed a decline in the vampire population?"

"I mean, not me specifically," she amended. "Neil's mentioned it one or two times."

"What does Neil have to do with vampires that he's noticed a decline in population?"

Her brow wrinkled, and she let Dante's shirt fall back into place. "You know, I really don't know.

"That's weird, Chris," I pointed out. "You are *marrying* this man."

"Correction: My father is marrying me to this man. Eventually. But right now, we need to get your friend patched up. Do I need to..." She waved a hand vaguely at the hole in my head. "Or will it just heal on its own?"

I fingered my gunshot wound. "It's already closing. It was twice as big when we left Bozeman."

Dante chuckled, then grimaced and croaked out, "I could see brain."

"No, you couldn't. Shut up, you've been shot," I told him. "Shouldn't you be unconscious?"

"L-O-L," he said ironically, closing his eyes.

While Christina left the room to gather supplies, I perched on the bed beside Dante and helped him get the rest of the now-destroyed t-shirt off over his head. There was a bit of huffing, puffing, and even some pained grunts, but I managed to free him from the cotton and then get him resting comfortably atop the covers.

"I'm going to have to buy her replacement bed clothes," Dante muttered, his eyes closed and a hand pressed to the skin just above his gunshot wound. Even covered in blood, pale with the loss of it, his torso made me think naughty things. I *really* wanted to clean every inch of it with my tongue. *But look at all my wondrous restraint.*

"They're hideous covers anyway," I told him. "I hate roses."

"No, you like sunflowers," he said.

I stared down at him, surprised he'd remembered that.

"We stopped in... Oh, man. Was it Calcutta?" he asked, opening his eyes to look at me. "You saw a field of them. I thought I'd never get you out of there. We were late to Mustafa's wedding. And you nicked one of those giant flowers right out of some poor farmer's land."

"I carried it for weeks, until it got so brown and shriveled that it disintegrated in my suitcase. I was picking sunflower bits out of my underwear for months after."

Dante smiled that sexy little half-quirk of his lips, then closed his eyes and asked, "If I drank one of your blood bags, would it replace some of what I lost?"

"Unfortunately, I don't think that's how blood transfusions work. But you're conscious, so I think you're okay. I'll cook you a rare steak for dinner. And after that..." I leaned over and nipped at his earlobe. "I'll do all the work."

He growled and turned his face into me, capturing my lips with his. I tried not to think about the fact that he'd lost his body weight in blood, and that I had a hole in my head as big around as a pen top, because those thoughts just weren't conducive to enjoying Dante Bloode's lips.

Christina cleared her throat from behind me, and I leapt away from the bed, heat rising in my cheeks. She raised a perfectly plucked eyebrow and slid past me carrying a large metal bowl of steaming water and several rags, with a first aid kit dangling off her elbow.

I flopped into the armchair in the corner to give her some room to work. I knew Christina had done several years of nursing school, though she hadn't ended up in the medical field. Those handy skills added to her air magic made her talented with healing craft, which was why I'd brought Dante here.

I watched her clean his two wounds, both entry and exit, while I told her what had happened. I couldn't tell her about Sarah. After all the trouble Hooper, Weaver & Sons had gone to to clean up our unintended mess, I didn't want to leave any loose ends. So, in the end, I made up a story about someone who'd contacted me asking to be changed to save their life, and put myself in the Corwin part of the story. Then I told her about my theory, and how Dante and I had gone into Bozeman to test it on dear ol' Hank. Thankfully, Christina didn't judge me for preying on a predator.

Though, still not my best hour.

But Christina was nothing if not a loyal friend. When I'd finished my sordid tale—detailing that I'd felt the oily magic on the fake friend instead of Sarah—I added, "I have a lot of questions, very few clues, and no answers. You got any advice?"

Christina straightened and rolled her shoulders as she said, "Could we back trace the victim's blood? Is any of this his?" She gestured to the soaked T-shirt on the floor by Dante.

"I had that thought of that, actually," I replied. "I have a vial of Hank's blood in my purse. Dante is a Bloode witch, so he can help me try that."

"Happily," Dante murmured.

"We can scan the blood for remnants of the original spell," Christina went on, turning back to the wound and reaching for her first aid kit. "If we can pinpoint a specific element as the basis, we can narrow down the witch families to see who could possibly be involved."

"Yeah, that's good. With wolfsbane and blooming nightshade?"

"Exactly. It's not a perfect spell, but it could tell us what kind of witch we're working with." Christina pulled a bottle of alcohol from the pack and soaked a fresh, clean rag. "You know, it makes sense, your theory that someone might have cursed vampires to be unable to sire. Vampires are already bound by so many parameters, not the least of which is being bound to the night. But magic helps you get around those pesky details. Just like magic could be used to make things even *worse* for you."

I shuddered, drawing my knees up to my chest and tugging the blanket off the back of the chair to cover my bare legs. The fact that I'd been right about our total loss of the ability to turn vampires didn't bring me any comfort or satisfaction. Sarah was still dead, and there wasn't a force in the universe that could bring her back.

As Christina sterilized Dante's wound and then set about stitching him up with deft fingers, I laid my head back on the edge of the chair and tried to organize my thoughts.

"What do you know about vampires?" I asked out loud.

"Other than my closest friend is one, and she's a pain in my ass?"

"Har, har."

Christina sighed. "Not much. I know that a Greene witch cursed them to be nightwalkers many centuries ago."

"A Greene witch," I said, "Like Gayle Greene."

"The one and the same family," Christina agreed. "It was a nasty curse. No one's been able to break it since, not even the Greene family. Borne of vengeance, they say. Legend stated a vampire did something horrific to her daughter, but I'm fuzzy on details."

"So, along those lines, we should expect that a vampire did something very bad to the witch who did this."

"Perhaps. I think sometimes, people just lose their minds and the tipping point could have been something as small as someone bumping into them on the subway." Christina pulled the needle back through and added, "Breathe, Dante. You're going to pass out."

I glanced at his face for the first time since she'd started sewing and realized his golden-tanned skin had gone white as a sheet. I slithered from the chair and went to his side, entwining my fingers in his hand.

"This population decline you mentioned..." I went on. "Did Neil tell you anything else other than 'gosh, there seem to be fewer vampires nowadays.'?"

Christina laughed. "That was an eerily accurate imitation of my fiance. Please don't ever do it again." We shared another laugh, but then her face fell into a thoughtful repose. "I don't recall exactly what he said. It was something with the Bureau of Magical Registration, and how there were no vampires registered in Shadow Hollow."

"I'm still registered as a witch. I never changed it. And Corwin refuses to register at all. I heard him get into it with the mayor a few months back." I rubbed my thumb over Dante's knuckles. "So is there just a lack of vampires in Shadow Hollow, or a lack everywhere?"

"I've never met one in L.A.," Dante spoke up, then sucked in another breath as Christina's needle pierced his skin one last time.

"L.A.?" Christina said, brow wrinkling. "There's no way a city *that* large doesn't have several hundred vampires running around draining bodies." Christina cut the end of the stitch string, then patted Dante on the thigh. "Alright, time to do the back side. Will, can you help him roll over?"

I took Dante by both hands and gently guided him into a roll. He must have been in immense pain, because I'd never seen him so pale, his face so contorted. Once he was settled on his stomach, his face turned toward me on the pillow, I knelt beside the bed so we were eye to eye and held his hand again.

"Are you sure?" I asked him as Christina opened a fresh sterile needle. "No vampires in LA?"

"I keep an eye out for them. Ever since your turn, I don't know, I guess I've been more sensitive to the fact they exist. I used to see them all the time back in Georgia, but I moved to L.A., what, two years ago? I haven't seen a single vamp." He sucked in a pained breath as Christina's needle dove back into his skin.

I slumped against the edge of the mattress with a groan. "That doesn't even make sense. L.A.? It should be vamp city. Something's up here, Christina. Someone's cursed the vampires of the world, and we're basically facing extinction at this point. What do I do?"

She glanced over at me. "Well, first of all, you calm down because the hole in your head is seeping dead blood, and it's alarming."

Dante snorted, his eyes flicking open so he could look, too.

I swiped my hand across the wound and made a face at the dead, clotted blood on my fingertips. "Being a vampire is not glamorous, I can tell you."

"I imagine it's not," Christina said soothingly, her gaze still firmly on Dante's exit wound as she sewed it shut. "I think a ritual is just the ticket to get us started on answers. I can't guarantee we'll figure it all out in the blink of an eye, but maybe we could find some new information."

"Is it going to be powerful enough with just the two of you to lead it?" I asked sullenly. Anytime the possibility of doing magic came up, I had a tendency to turn petulant.

"I don't think it will, unfortunately," Christina said. "Would you be amenable to sharing your secret with some of the cov—"

"No," I cut in. "Absolutely not. I'm not telling the coven I'm a vampire and ruining the good thing I have going with them."

"But we need three, maybe four more people, preferably blooded witches..."

"I can get some people," Dante spoke up. His long,

dark lashes fluttered open, and he looked at me. "It would be male witches. Bloodes. I know you Goodes are obsessed with the whole matriarchal line thing, but Bloodes are all I have to offer."

I leaned in and kissed him on the nose. "That would be perfect. I won't even complain about the testosterone clogging up the ritual space. What else would we need?" I asked Christina. "We don't have anything to connect us to the original curse caster. No talisman, no lock of hair. We're working blind."

"We are," Christina agreed with a thoughtful nod, "but I think there's a work around. The Librarian keeps an extensive list of occult tomes in his private collection. He's an avid collector. I'm not his biggest fan, but I think we need one of his books."

"Okay, what do I do to get it?"

"Go to the library and ask to see the Librarian's special collection."

"That's it? No blood to pay or anything? Just 'hey, can I borrow a book?'"

"Well..." Christina stared at Dante's wound a little harder than necessary. "Some people say he's... I've heard he has a price."

"What kind of price?"

Christina shrugged. "I don't really know. Just... be careful. Okay?"

"I'm always careful," I assured her.

I mean, what could possibly go wrong at a public library?

CHAPTER

SIX

I didn't wake up alone the next morning, since Dante's furnace-burning body was curled up against mine, but the cottage felt as empty as the grave.

I lay curled in the circle of Dante's arms for several long moments without moving. The clock on my bedside table read just past seven. On a normal day—normal being that my best friend wasn't dead—I'd hear her puttering around the kitchen. The smell of bacon and eggs would permeate the hallway, seeping right under the crack in my door to spur me out of bed earlier than my typical time. The gentle clink of last night's dinner dishes in the sink as she washed them. Little meows as Castor and Pollux begged for treats. All of it the music of my life with Sarah.

But this morning dawned cold and silent. Yet

another reminder of her absence and what it meant to be gone forever.

I slithered over Dante's sleeping form, careful not to jostle his injured side or wake him. I didn't see any reason for him to wake up to go with me to the library. Less than twenty-four hours had passed since he was shot and lost enough blood to turn him into Casper the Friendly Ghost. I wanted him to stay right where he was in the warmth of my bed and recuperate.

In the kitchen, I brewed some coffee, making sure enough would be left behind for Dante when he finally struggled out of bed. While the brewer did its little gurgle routine, I filled up Castor and Pollux's bowls, then took several moments to love all over both of them. They'd noticed Sarah's absence within hours of Hooper, Weaver & Sons removing her body for the wake. Since then, they'd wandered the house, crying and restless. I hated to see it, because it seemed like they were grieving no less than me. At some point, we'd have decisions to make. What to do with Sarah's house. Where the cats would go.

I couldn't deal with that alone. Corwin would have to come out of hiding sooner or later.

After a quick shower, I dabbed some concealer over the bruise on my forehead where the gunshot wound had healed over, wondering how on earth I'd become the kind of woman who could say she'd survived a gunshot wound to the head. Then I dressed in some skinny jeans and a bell-sleeved peasant blouse, before grabbing my leather jacket and heading out the door.

The Shadow Hollow Library sat close to the main square but on the southern edge with a breathtaking view of the Crazy Mountains. It was the only building in town with Greco-Roman architecture, sporting wide white columns so big around even a grown man couldn't hug them, and a soaring rotunda that arched high over the quiet street. I'd seen the place dozens of times driving between Sarah's cottage and the downtown area, but I'd never personally set foot inside.

I found an empty spot on the street and dropped a quarter in the machine, then hurried up the sidewalk, hunching my shoulders against the autumn chill. Shadow Hollow typically had beautiful weather, especially through the spring and summer months, but fall came on quick and came on fast, and once we hit December, the wind would cut like knives.

I skipped up the wide, shallow front steps to the library, stepping aside to let another patron exit with a stack of books in her arms before I slipped inside the uber-modern chrome and glass doors. I'd expected more columns, more stone, more of that ancient Greek temple feel, but the inside of the library did *not* match the outside. The only stone was the arched rotunda overhead, decorated with skylights instead of artwork, and the grand staircase at the back of the main room that was roped off with a little yellow sign that stated *Staff Access Only*.

I glanced around, noting the bank of public computers already occupied by early risers, and the orderly stacks sweeping out in all directions from the central atrium. Then I picked my jaw up off the floor and sidled up to the circulation desk.

"Hi!" I said cheerfully to the woman behind the counter. I squinted at her nametag - a little square of blue with a gold silhouette of a buffalo and the name *Lulu*. "I need to make an appointment to see the Librarian."

Lulu looked up from the stack of books she was carefully scanning into her computer system. Her movements faltered, the kid's book she held hanging in mid-air beneath the radar gun. "You want to see the Librarian?"

I blinked, then said, "Uh. Yeah? Is he not in?"

She was a gorgeous girl, with her dark hair in a high-top fade, lightning bolts cut into the stubble above her ears, but maybe she wasn't that bright considering the way she stared at me like I'd lost my mind.

"He's always in," she replied cryptically.

She ducked behind the counter, disappearing so entirely I thought she'd fallen through the floor. I leaned over to search for her, then leapt back as she reappeared just as quickly, dropping a giant book on the counter in front of me.

"This is his appointment book," she said. "You sign, indicate what you need help with, and then we'll call you when he's ready to see you. Be ready to come the moment we call. The Librarian doesn't like to be kept waiting."

"What is he, a mafia don?" I joked, picking up a pen.

Lulu slapped the Bic out of my hand and offered me an honest-to-gods feather quill. "This one."

She opened the book to a page covered in lines. Six of the lines on the left-hand page had already been filled in, and she tapped the next available space with a long red fingernail.

The woman was legitimately acting like I was signing over my soul. Considering I'd already done that when I became a vampire, there was nothing this Librarian could take from me, so he didn't scare me.

Clearly, though, he scared Lulu.

I scrawled out my whole name, then added "special collections" as my note on what I needed. I passed the feather quill back to Lulu, and she slammed the book shut.

"We'll call you when he's ready."

"Any kind of time frame?" I asked.

But before she could reply, a new voice piped in from behind me. "How about now?"

I whipped around to find an elegant, old-fashioned man standing with his legs together and a cane propped beneath both hands. He wore black pants and a satiny pirate shirt, and his hair fell just past his ears in delicate feathers that framed his squat, pointed face. Despite being much older than me, I still found him oddly handsome, in a pulled-from-the-pages-of-a-Regency-romance kind of way.

He nodded his head once. "Willow Goode. It's a pleasure. I'm Earl Harris, the Head Librarian of this establishment."

I had the oddest urge to curtsy but refrained. "Nice to meet you. So you're free to meet with me now?"

"Indeed. Follow me."

He whirled around and marched towards the grand staircase. I cast one more glance at Lulu to find her staring after him with an odd, almost fearful expression, then hurried to keep up.

Earl Harris unhooked the *Staff Access Only* sign and motioned for me to precede him, then replaced it and took the lead again. The stairs were carpeted in lush purple shot through with creamy curlicues that reminded me of the ancient era-appropriate curtains at my Aunt Mags' antebellum farm. He led me up the stairs and then we took a right down the hallway.

WE ENDED up in a little room at the very end of the hallway that looked as if it were meant to be a reading room. Several cushioned armchairs were scattered about the hardwood floor, and a fire burned in the grate inside a magnificently crafted marble fireplace. A row of long, narrow windows in the back wall looked out over the mountains like some kind of multimillion dollar movie set. Sometimes, I couldn't believe the beauty of this area was real.

"Please, have a seat, Miss Goode." Earl paused beside an armchair and held out a hand, indicating I should sit in the one opposite.

I complied, but not without asking, "How do you know my name?"

Earl smoothed his pants down in the back before sitting primly on his chair. He propped his cane against the side arm and then brushed his hair from his face before finally regarding me with what seemed like an almost haughty air.

"My job is to know everything about this town, Miss Goode," he said. "For example, I also know you're a vampire."

I gasped, my hands clasping into fists in my lap. "Nobody knows that."

"On the contrary, a fair few of your friends do know, and as such, it becomes basic knowledge for my purposes." He settled against the back of the chair and crossed his legs, eying me for a few uncomfortable moments. "Tell me, Miss Goode. What need does a vampire have from the library's special collections?"

I jolted again. "How did you know what I need—"

Earl held up a hand to stop me. "We've already discussed this. I know things. It's my job."

"Then shouldn't you already know Christina Steele sent me here for a specific book from your collection?" I shot back.

One of his pointed eyebrows rose towards his hairline. "If you'd like my help, I'd suggest speaking to me with a little more respect."

Inwardly, I ranted and screamed like a little bitch. Outwardly, I just shrugged and said, "Sorry."

"Which book?"

I dug my phone out of my bag and opened the note-taking app where I'd marked down the title Christina had given me. "The *Veritas Daemonium*?"

"You don't say," Harris said, clearly intrigued. "Why don't you start from the beginning and tell me just what you need with this tome, and then I'll decide whether or not to grant you access."

It took me about ten minutes and several confusing turnarounds to get the whole story out. I bypassed any mention of Sarah completely, and used the same story I'd given Christina about my "friend" in Bozeman. I laid out my theories about a possible witch curse, thanks to the oily feeling of black magic on "his" dead body. And I explained how Christina believed the *Veritas Daemonium* had a spell inside that could help us trace the source of the curse to find answers.

When I was finished, Harris was stroking his smooth chin, a thoughtful look on his pointed face. "Very interesting. Young Miss Steele is right, though, of course, she would know. The *Veritas Daemonium* is a highly powerful book of truth spells. Highly powerful... and highly dangerous."

I filed away his mysterious *she would know* for later

as proof that Christina was hiding something from me. "I'm really good with magic. Or I was, before…" I trailed off. "Anyway, Christina's really good. And we're going to have a coven of Bloode witches to help us."

"Ah. Bloode witches. My favorite." Harris flashed a wicked grin. "You know, Miss Goode, I do think you're onto something. I, too, haven't seen many vampires in recent months. I had a dear colleague, William Drake; the man must have been eight hundred, nine hundred years old… He was a rare books supplier, and one I often called on. Never missed my call. Never didn't *return* my call. He vanished off the grid last summer. I could only assume something terrible had happened, of course, as is the way for supernatural creatures. But now…"

"You agree it could have been a curse?" I asked, excited for somebody else to see the possibility laid out so neatly.

"The idea has merit," he said. "If we couple William's disappearance with the strange, dark power I felt sweep through Shadow Hollow that same month…"

"Dark power?"

He inclined his head. "Something dark and vengeful. Honestly, I didn't think much of it. I'm sensitive to energies like that, particularly in my town, and a good curse is cast every few years. But if you're correct, that could have been the curse that doomed vampires. I haven't seen another since, beyond you and Mr. Pitts."

"That's funny," I mused. "I have a friend who says there are no vampires in L.A. And Christina is certain she hasn't seen one come to Shadow Hollow in months."

Harris paused, the skin between his brows knotting in thought. "Tell me, Miss Goode, when were you turned?"

"Last year."

"When?"

"Um, I think..." I thought back, trying to piece together those last few days. I'd been diagnosed with ALS on June eleventh, which meant I was turned... "The thirteenth of June."

"As I thought. I felt this dark force sweep through Shadow Hollow in November. Whatever curse was cast, you were already a vampire."

"What's your point?"

"Well, we can assume, of course, that the curse removed your ability to turn new vampires," Harris said. "But that hardly explains William's disappearance, or your friend's absolute belief that there are no vampires in L.A. What if this curse put an end to all vampires?"

"But then why am I still here? And Corwin?"

"Think very carefully, Miss Goode. Witches can take away, but witches can give, as well. Daywalker charms, protection against enemies, etcetera. Could you have been protected?"

A hand fluttered to my lips. "Yes, actually," I said,

dropping my hand back to my lap as my surprise tingled through me. "Corwin and I both. Sarah did extensive protection spells on us. I mean, she was almost maniacal about it, especially after I was turned and lost my powers."

"As I thought. I would imagine, Miss Goode, that you survived this curse thanks to your friend Sarah. As did Mr. Pitts." He leaned forward, his arms resting on the arms of his chair. "In fact, I want to help you, because I'm eager to solve this interesting conundrum. Come. We have to go beneath the library."

We left behind the reading room and its bright cheerful windows for a small service elevator down the hall. Harris and I remained mute as the cage rattled and creaked its way below ground, and when we banged into the floor, he opened the grate and led me into the bowels of hell.

Okay, not really, but it totally felt like it.

The cramped, narrow hallway ended at a vast basement room filled with overflowing stacks. Harris hit a switch on the wall that illuminated faux torches all around the space one by one, giving the whole place an atmospheric, Harry Potter vibe.

"I cannot touch the *Veritas Daemonium*," he said, leading me with his odd shuffling gait down the central aisle. "And in order for the cage to open, you'll have to give blood."

"I'm not afraid of a little blood," I said with a shrug. "Wait—cage?"

He ignored me. We bypassed all of the free-standing stacks for the back wall of the room, where dozens of little alcoves held single books behind iron gates. Harris stopped before a gate on the far left, about waist high, then tugged a small pen knife from his pocket and offered it to me.

"You don't need much. I know your blood is slower than most."

I nodded. *No time like the present*, I thought, and sliced the knife across my palm before I pressed it to the keyhole on the gate.

A flash of red blinded me, and I tossed up an arm to cover my eyes. Then a metallic click heralded the gate opening on slow, creaky hinges.

"You must return it within the week," Harris said, motioning for me to take the *Veritas*. "These books have strict deadlines; holding it over its agreed upon return could have disastrous consequences."

I hefted the book out of its tiny cage, surprised by the meaty weight of it between my hands. The cover looked to be leather, carved with dozens of strange sigils I didn't recognize.

"Is this a witch grimoire?" I asked.

Harris chuckled. "It is a book of demon magic."

Startled, I almost dropped the damn thing as if it were made of flames but caught it at the last minute and clutched it to my chest. "*Demon* magic?"

"Indeed. Any spell you choose to perform from it will require a blood sacrifice and a sacred talisman to activate the magic. The talisman, ideally, should be organic."

I shifted the book's odd weight to my hip. "Organic? Like kombucha?"

"No, Miss Goode. Organic as in once of the living. Like bone or hair."

My skin grew cold, and I could just sense Aunt Mags doing the pissed-off conga in her grave.

Because I had a sacred talisman made of organic matter. The Goode reliquary. A necklace formed of dozens of tiny bones.

Temperance Goode's bones.

CHAPTER

SEVEN

When Aunt Mags bequeathed Temperance Goode's reliquary to me, I doubt she planned on me using it to perform demon magic. In fact, there was a good chance that the minute I pulled out the bones and let the Bloode witches have them, she'd show up in all her dead-and-gone glory and beat me thoroughly with a switch.

But desperate times, desperate measures, and all that jazz. Family tradition couldn't really stand up against vengeance curses and mass genocide.

I leaned a hip on the edge of the doorframe and looked in at Dante. He was awake, but still in bed, propped up against the pillows while he scrolled on his phone. He was wearing *glasses*, delicate wire frames perched on the edge of his nose, and he looked ridiculously wholesome. I liked this side of him almost as much as I liked the leather and chrome side.

"How's your hole?" I asked.

He closed his phone screen and looked over at me. "Feels like I swallowed fire."

"You ready for the next round of painkillers?"

"Not if I'm going to take part in the ritual." He rotated ever so slightly off the edge of the mattress, hissing in pain as he dropped his feet to the floor. I crossed to him in three strides, and took his hands to help him stand so that he didn't have to carry the brunt of his weight.

"You could sit it out," I suggested.

"Like hell." He got his balance on his bare feet, then brushed his hands back through my hair, gazing down at me with something a lot like affection. "The guys are on the way. Should be here in about an hour. They managed to sweet talk a local faery into letting them cross through the ley lines."

I leaned against him and wrapped my arms around his waist, careful to keep my weight and my body away from his injury. "I don't know what any of that means, but okay."

"Is there any food in this joint?" Dante asked, leaning down to press a quick kiss to my forehead. "I'm famished."

I wasn't exactly a domestic goddess, so I dropped a couple waffles in the toaster and plastered them in butter and syrup for him. Once he was installed at the kitchen table with his freezer breakfast and a fresh mug of black coffee, I decided it was time to stop putting off retrieving the reliquary.

I unlatched the door to the basement and flipped the switch at the top of the stairway. I hadn't been back here since the night Sarah died, and just standing at the top of the stairs, looking down into the dim abyss, recalled a dozen strong emotions, none of them good. The smell of strong bleach drifted up from below, though, beneath that, I could still smell the blood.

Blood was never really gone, even when you couldn't see it anymore.

My few storage boxes were piled in a corner in the main room downstairs, thankfully on the opposite side of the basement from the room where Sarah died. But despite the fact I could avoid that room, all of Sarah's things released a flood of emotions I wasn't equipped to deal with.

The basement screamed Sarah's entire life. A shelving unit weighed down beneath jar goods, many of which Sarah had canned herself. A corner of large tupperware containers marked for the holidays: *Christmas, Halloween, Easter*. There were photo albums on the table, books stacked haphazardly on the floor, a dozen years of Sarah's life in bits and pieces all around.

It was too much. My vision had gone wavy, and my eyes grew hot. I flopped into an overstuffed chair, loosening some of the stuffing where the cats had shredded the side, and the tears came. I wept away my grief, my guilt, my anger. I fell into every emotion and sensation I had, everything I'd tried to medicate with gin or tried to ignore with my need to find answers. For a while, it was just me and my love for Sarah, who I'd never, ever get back.

But someone once said that grief was a passage, not somewhere you should stay. Hazel had parroted that to me so many times during Aunt Mags' funeral rites, and I'd clung to it as an absolute. Fall into the grief. Let the emotion pass through you. Deal with it.

Then pull up your gods-damned bootstraps and get on with the damn thing.

Temperance Goode's reliquary wasn't in the first box I checked, but I found it shoved down inside the second box, wrapped in an old rabbit fur with a quartz crystal for cleansing. I tossed the fur and the crystal back inside the box, then looked down at the necklace, thinking how weird it was that I held some woman's finger bones in my palm.

The human hand had twenty-seven bones, and each of them formed a shaved pearl on the necklace. Both of Temperance's hands, hands that had saved lives, cast curses, cleaned up messes. Hands that had made a difference and hands that had picked and chosen who would live and who would die. I could almost feel the necklace hum with power, though perhaps it was just a memory of what it had felt like a year ago, before the vampire neutered me.

Either way, I clasped the necklace around my neck and headed back upstairs. We had a ritual to catch.

Christina opened her front door before I could even knock, and the look on her face said, *I am not happy with you, Willow Goode.*

"What's going on?" I asked hesitantly, my hand still hovering in the air as if I were gonna beat down her door. In reality, I was ready to turn tail and run for the hills at that look on her face.

"The Bloode witches are here," she said stiffly, tossing a glance over her shoulder. As if on cue, I heard something shatter somewhere near the back of the house, and then a chorus of laughter followed.

Dante grinned. "They're a handful, I know. Best warlocks you'll ever meet, though."

"No doubt," Christina said wryly and stepped aside to let us pass into the house.

I was used to being in Christina's house when it was jam-packed with the Crazy Woman Coven. They weren't, as advertised, "crazy." The moniker came from the Crazy Mountains, which were originally called the Crazy Woman Mountains. Crow legend stated that the mountains were named for a woman whose family was decimated by westward settling pioneers. She went mad from their loss and hid deep in the mountains, thus giving them their name.

When the coven formed many moons ago, they'd wanted to honor the flavor of the area. Reclaiming the Crazy Woman name had seemed right at the time, and they'd stuck with it.

Now, however, Christina's house was overflowing with Bloode men instead of crazy women.

I stopped in the doorway to the kitchen, gaping at the ten men positioned around the room. Clearly, there was something in the water when it came to Bloode men, because every last one of them was tall, dark, and delicious. They ran the gamut of ages, some of them appearing to be upwards of their late thirties, and one who looked as young as a teenager. But they all shared quite a few characteristics, like Dante's strong jaw, that dark hair that seemed too shiny to be real, and skin that tanned if the sun even peeked through the clouds.

Dante leaned in, his lips brushing my ear. "You're gawking."

"You didn't tell me there were more of you."

"Babe, there's only one of me, and you know it." His lips trailed further down my neck, and his breath fanned over my collarbone, sending delectable shivers down my spine.

Yeah. He was right. There could only be one Dante Bloode, and he knew how to push all my buttons.

Suddenly, all the little Bloodes noticed Dante's arrival. The noise level reached altitudes even planes couldn't fly, and Christina and I backed out of the room, leaving him to the masses.

Christina sighed and turned her back on the tableau of Bloodes, pinching the bridge of her nose. "They've been driving me crazy for an hour. Can we go ahead and get this started? The last thing I need is for all of them to still be here when Neil gets home." Her gaze dropped to my collarbone, visible since I'd chosen to wear a gauzy tank top and blue jeans. "Is that it?"

I nodded, reaching around to unclasp the reliquary. "One necklace made of human bones," I murmured, letting it fall into Christina's outstretched hand.

She made a face. "Ew. As grossed out as I am, I imagine this will do nicely."

"Nothing will happen to it. Right?"

Christina shrugged, giving me an apologetic grimace. "I don't know, Will. I've never done demon magic before."

I wanted to ask her, *Then how did you know about the Veritas Daemonium? And what did Earl Harris mean by "she would know"?* But I held my tongue. Even I had my secrets. It wasn't fair to demand she spill all her dark and twisted things if I wasn't going to do the same.

Dante sidled back to me and wrapped an arm around my shoulders. "You ladies ready to do this? The guys are raring to go."

As a group, we all tramped downstairs to the ritual

space Christina had built into her basement. She'd spared no expense, placing a permanent copper circle in her floor and equipping the central altar with everything we'd ever need for ritual. Four cardinal points were painted on the floor, cabinets lined the walls with ritual supplies. There was a place for everything and everything in its place.

Except that was the norm for the Crazy Woman Coven. With eleven Bloode men taking up all the air in the room, nothing seemed to be in place at all.

Christina opened the *Veritas Daemonium* and paged forward to where she'd marked a passage with a scrap of paper she'd clearly taken notes on. I'd dropped the book to her that morning on my way back home. She passed the paper to me, then tapped her finger on the spell written in oddly red ink. "This is dangerous, Will. But I think it's our only option."

I leaned over to read the heading at the top of the page. "A demon summoning? Holy Hades, Christina, are you out of your mind?"

"Not out of my mind, no," she said with a weary smile. "Just out of ideas. I dug through *all* the Steele witch grimoires I own last night, and I found nothing that could help us trace the curse backwards. It'd be easier if we had something of the original witch's, like a lock of hair or some kind of object she used in ritual, such as a crystal or a talisman. But we don't even know who she was, so this is what we're left with."

"A demon summoning," I repeated, still aghast.

Dante peered over my shoulder at the spell, his blue gaze raking over it so quickly, I couldn't believe he'd even read it. "It seems fairly straight forward. I've done summonings before. As long as you do it safely, calling the demon in a circle of salt and keeping them there the whole time, they can't hurt us."

Christina picked up a giant jar of Morton salt and held it out to me. "It's our one choice right now, Will. Take it or leave it."

I snatched the salt out of her hand with an irritated snarl. "Fine. But I don't have to like it."

While I took my time pouring a perfect circle of salt in the middle of the copper ritual circle, Christina worked on herding Bloodes into place and preparing everyone for ritual. She was such a pro at magic, and such a pro at bossing people around, that we were ready to bring in the demon within ten minutes. Much too soon for my anxiety, which had reached a state of turmoil I'd previously never known.

I joined Christina at the altar for the opening incantation. Despite her calm, even voice, my nerves were rattled. Dante's presence at my back couldn't even chase away the chill I felt, and I wondered if we were doing the right thing. I knew without a doubt if Aunt Mags—or hell, even Hazel—knew I was using Temperance Goode's bones to summon a demon, they'd lose their minds.

Christina picked up a tiny knife and turned to me.

"Do you want to cut your own hand or do you want me to do it?"

I plucked the knife from her fingers and slid it across my palm, hiding the flinch with a minor twitch of my right eye. Christina took hold of my palm and held it over the candle flame, palm down, before reciting something in Latin.

Ugh. Latin. Any spell written in Latin couldn't be good.

Despite my misgivings over the type of ritual, I hated being a minor player in the drama. I had no magic to contribute, no power to filter into the circle and boost the summoning. So I stood silently—maybe even a little petulantly—at Christina's side and listened to her speak the Latin incantations with more confidence than I ever would have had.

Christina's voice gained power, and the incantation turned to a chant. She motioned for the Bloode witches to pick up the chant with her, and their voices rose in tandem with hers. I swayed gently, my eyes closing as the chant turned to music. The melody became all I knew, and all I'd ever known. Their voices the siren song, their magic my everything.

Then a flash of light burst through the room, and a puff of smoke filtered through the circle of salt. When it faded, the circle was no longer empty.

The being that occupied the space hadn't manifested in a physical body. He was semi-translucent, glowing from the inside out with skin that smoldered in shades of red and black like hardening lava beneath his sharp three piece suit and satin cravat. He had dark hair, slicked back over his head, a pointed chin, and a widow's peak that gave him an almost cartoonish villain look. His forked tongue darted out between thick, red lips, and his eyes burned like fire as he regarded us.

His fiery gaze caught mine. "Why do you summon me?"

I glanced at Christina, my mouth suddenly dry. "Um. We're seeking answers."

"You wish to know about the curse that put an end to the vampires," he said smoothly.

I glared. "If you knew that, why did you ask me?"

"I don't freely give information, child. Summoning me doesn't get you what you want. I require respect," he said, then a slow smile spread across his face. "I require payment."

My sluggish, undead heart raised its head and gave a few half-hearted thuds. "What payment?"

"Your soul."

I burst out laughing. "Honey, I don't have a soul to give you. Nice try, though." I pointed at my chest. "Vampire."

The demon clasped his hands in front of him, his head tilting curiously. "You act as if I did not know already, child. I did. And you do indeed have a soul. When your earthly form as a vampire ends, your soul will be released from the purgatory where it waits. At that time, I wish to have it."

"For what purpose?"

"Let's say… research," the demon replied, grin widening.

"Willow! Don't you dare," Dante hissed from behind me. He couldn't break ranks on the circle to come to me, though I could sense his underlying desire to do so.

But if I *did* still have a soul somewhere, it was mine and mine alone. As such, it meant it was mine to give away, too. Plus, let's be honest, I was a *vampire*. I had no intentions of dying any time soon. And if I signed over my soul now, perhaps I could come up with a contingency plan. Something to keep me safe in the unlikely event of my death.

"Fine. You can have it," I said flippantly. "Now tell me who cast the curse that thrust vampires into extinction."

"A white witch," he intoned. "One from a long, distinguished line. She carried a vendetta like nothing Hell has ever seen."

"What's her name?"

"That I cannot tell you."

I crossed my arms over my tank top. "Then I rescind the agreement to give you my soul."

He raised an eyebrow. "As if it is so easy, child. You humans, always caught up in the black and white. The good and evil. Answers and mystery."

"You're not making any sense."

"Or perhaps you're not meant to understand," he shot back, striding right up the edge of the circle. "There are things I can tell you and things I cannot, as the laws of Hell bind me. I cannot reveal her name to you. Yet I can give you some knowledge."

"Then enlighten me, o great one," I said.

"Your mother's biggest passion in the year before her untimely death had much to do with the vampires' future and how witch magic affects them." He straightened, seeming to loom even higher. The flames in his eyes burned like hot coals. "Seek your answers there, and you will be led to the truth."

Then the demon burst into flames and disappeared—setting the whole gods damned room on fire.

EIGHT

Christina's reflexes were to die for. She picked up the bowl of water we'd used in casting the circle and flung it at the flames licking around the summoning circle. A sheet of salty water sprayed over the floor. Fire sizzled and white smoke filled the room, and one of the Bloode men grabbed a tapestry off the wall to pat out the rest of the flames.

I stood next to the altar, immobile, staring down at the soot-blackened floor. The strong smell of brimstone lingered. A white witch with a vendetta. Gods, those were dime a dozen, weren't they? At one time, I was probably a white witch with a vendetta, too.

Christina stepped up beside me, her dark gaze sweeping over the ruined floor, before she looked up at the Bloode men. "Gentlemen, please go and help yourselves to the food and drink waiting in the kitchen. You need to recuperate from such a powerful working."

The Bloodes murmured their agreement and tramped up the wooden steps, sounding like a charging horde of bulls. Dante joined us at the altar, where smoke still curled up from the floor.

"Well. That was a whole lot of nothing," Dante said.

Christina bent down and lifted the smoking tapestry to survey the damage. "We know more than we knew this morning."

"A white witch with a vendetta tells us fuck all," I muttered, kicking at the blackened salt that had held the demon in.

"No, it doesn't." Christina draped her ruined tapestry over a nearby metal folding chair then clasped her hands behind her back and caught my eye. "But the part about your mom does."

"What did he say again?" Dante asked.

Christina parroted the demon's words. "Your mother's biggest passion in the year before her untimely death had much to do with the vampires' future and how witch magic affects them."

I finally turned away from the damage and stalked past the altar, my thoughts awhirl. "What would my mom have to do with vampires? I'd never even met one until I moved here and met Corwin. They weren't exactly out and proud in the American south."

Christina grabbed my elbow as I paced past her for

the second time, and she drew me to a halt. Clutching both my shoulders in her hands, she said, "Just because you didn't know vampires doesn't mean your mom didn't. She had a whole life before you showed up."

"I guess. But what do we do now?"

Dante spoke up. "We scry."

Christina and I turned as one to raise confused eyebrows at him.

He grinned. "Come on. Scrying is one of the things Bloodes do best. And Goodes aren't half bad at it, either."

Christina nodded, a thoughtful look touching her expression. "What are we scrying for?"

Dante tapped his knuckles on the altar as he considered the question, but I answered first.

"We look back into my mother's life," I said. "Look for any clues about work she might have done with vampires, or research, or whatever."

Christina nodded. "Okay. How do we do that?"

"There's a Bloode conjuration," Dante offered. "All we need is something that belonged to the individual and blood from her bloodline."

"I have both," I said simply, touching my earrings. "These were Mom's. And gods know I look just like her, so it's definitely her blood running through my veins. As, well, *undead* as it is today."

"Actually, that might make the spell even stronger," Dante said excitedly. "We're looking for memories about vampires, and you're now a vampire. The tie is there."

"Tenuous at best," I said with a laugh.

Dante slipped a hand around my waist and tugged me in for a kiss that made my toes curl. "Trust me, babe. I'm just the witch you need."

He pulled away, leaving my insides just as smokin' hot as Christina's poor floor, and I thought, *Whoo, boy, you sure are* just *what I need.*

It took us half an hour to set the ritual space to rights after the demon's flambe exit, but we finally got the basement cleared of lingering smoke and the scent of brimstone, thanks to five open windows and an industrial strength fan.

Dante set to work lighting thirteen white candles in a circle around the altar. I stared down at the black glass mirror Christina had pulled out of the storage closet. It was three square feet of midnight and hung over the edge of the altar precariously. My reflection was in shades of gray, like an artist's charcoal rendition of my face, and my nerves had settled in nicely.

"You okay?" Christina asked gently, nudging me with her elbow as she lit a black candle in the center of the mirror.

I swallowed, and the shadowy girl in the mirror

did the same. "Just... seeing my mom again, you know? I was young when she died."

Christina slid the match book onto the shelf beneath the altar's tabletop. "If you don't want to do this, we can find another way."

I shook my head. "It's not a terrible idea. Painful, maybe, to see her again and know she's gone. But if Dante says he can conjure up my mama's memories for answers, I trust him."

A sly smile crossed her pretty face, and she tossed Dante a look before lowering her voice. "You *like* this guy, don't you?"

I flushed, heat snaking up my neck and into my cheeks. Thank the gods for my natural tan. "Don't make an epic event out of it."

Dante appeared as if out of nowhere, and I jumped, letting out a ridiculously out of character squeak. He raised an eyebrow at me, then asked, "You ladies ready?"

I nodded and wished the raging inferno in my cheeks would die down already. Dante had *never* affected me like this before. I mean, sure, the whole lust thing was pretty incredible, and even the thought of a shirtless Dante was enough to rev my engines, but this weird little schoolgirl crush was all new territory.

"Make a triangle," Dante said, holding out one hand to me and one hand to Christina.

We positioned ourselves around the mirror, facing one another in an estimation of a triangle. In witchcraft, the triangle was a revered symbol due to the fact it had three sides, and three was the most magical number.

Dante began to hum—a low, deep sound that wouldn't have been out of place in a monk's temple. And I'd been to a few of those in my world travels. He kept the note going and his eyes closed for several moments. I split my attention between him and Christina, whose serene face calmed my anxiety. I almost thought I could feel magic tingling in my fingers and all around me, but it was just wishful thinking.

Dante's hum cut off, and he began to chant. "Bind our power over the past, as our hands and minds join fast. Mirror, we beseech you speak. Show us the Goode witch whom we seek. A moment of her life, now history, and the answer we need to solve the mystery."

I wondered what Dante's power felt like. Where the Steeles were air witches and the Goodes were fire witches, the Bloodes were spirit witches. But spirit wasn't so much a tangible element, so I was dying to know how his magic tasted on the air. How powerful could we have been together in ritual magic, if I hadn't given up my powers for eternal life?

Not exactly something I'd take back, anyway, but the thought remained.

Dante spoke again. "Will, I need you to visualize your mother. As close to life as possible. Think of her favorite things and places. And while you're doing that, think of vampires."

He started up the humming note again, and I closed my eyes to obey his instructions. I could easily conjure an image of my mother in my mind. I pictured one of my favorite memories - me, Mama, and Hazel sitting on Aunt Mags' big ol' wraparound porch. Mama reading to us from a book, the door standing open so we could hear Mags puttering around in the kitchen and smell the delicious scents coming from her cooking.

Mama wore black leggings and an oversized t-shirt tied at the hip. She was short and curvy like me, with dark hair and eyes and the most infectious smile like I've never seen since.

Then I thought of Corwin, and the mystery of the extinct vampires. What was Mama up to? Or did the demon lie to me? *Show me*, I begged the mirror. *Please*.

Christina gasped. "Something's happening."

I opened my eyes and looked down at the black mirror, my undead heart trying its damndest to wake up and express my excitement. At first, I didn't see anything but my own shadowy face staring back at me, and the tops of Christina and Dante's heads.

But then I saw movement.

The glass swirled with a light mist, like fog coming in off the ocean. It filled the whole square, turning the mirror into a black and white Jackson Pollock painting, while little golden sparkles darted around like stars winking.

Dante leaned over and blew on the mirror.

Immediately, the fog cleared, revealing a woman.

My mother.

I leaned in for a better look, still clutching my friends' hands. Mama stood on a cracked, weed-choked sidewalk at twilight, glancing around a clearing as if fearful someone might have followed her. In the distance behind her, I saw thick woods and a rising moon, but her immediate surroundings were a grassy field with a small hill jutting out of the dirt in front of her.

No... not a hill. The bunker. Dad's bunker.

My father had been a mechanic, which was where my sister got her love of cars from. Being a mechanic, of course, was fairly normal. Where he fell a little short of sane was in his apocalyptic prepping mentality.

Daddy believed the world was gonna end, and it was gonna end *soon*. He bought a bunker in the woods from some old guy when I was an infant, and then spent the next ten years filling it with canned goods, gallons of water, and ammo.

Mama thought it was cute, and Hazel got into the spirit of things, helping him stock the shelves every chance she got. Me? I thought he was kooky-do. But I loved him dearly. And I did love the bunker itself because it felt like a secret hideaway.

In this scene, however, Mama was alone. She

looked tired, with dark circles under her eyes and her hair pulled into a haphazard bun that had slipped a bit around her face. She drew a key ring from the pocket of her coat and unlocked the bunker door, before slipping inside.

"Is that her?" Dante whispered.

I nodded, not trusting myself to speak.

Mama walked down the steep, narrow staircase that led twelve feet below the surface. A light was already on downstairs, glowing like a beacon in the dark tunnel, and my first thought was, *Oh, Daddy must be there, too.*

Except why would Daddy be locked inside the bunker while Mama had the key?

When she stepped off the last stair, the room opened up ahead of her, as familiar as the last time I saw it. About half the size of a football field, lined with metal shelves absolutely weighed down by products. There was a kitchenette in a far corner and bunk beds in another. All of it was illuminated by irritatingly bright fluorescents.

There was a man on one of the bunk beds. A man that wasn't my daddy.

He was long and wiry, like the gods had stretched him a little too much before putting him in the oven, and one of those skinny arms was shackled to the metal bed frame. He rolled off the bottom mattress and hissed at Mama, baring two sharp canines. His T-shirt and jeans had seen cleaner days, and his vividly green eyes were half-crazed. He scrambled away from Mama on all fours, backing between the two bunk beds.

"Shh, no, it's okay," Mama cooed, pulling her satchel around to her front side. She reached into the bag and extracted a bag of blood, like what Corwin got at the blood bank. "I brought dinner."

The man unfolded his lanky form from between the beds and stood, chains clanking. He took a single step forward, crazy eyes locked on the blood bag.

Mama held it out at arm's length.

He shrieked and darted backwards, as if afraid Mama would hit him.

Her somewhat hopeful expression fell away, and she tossed the blood bag at his feet. "You need to eat."

He stared at her for a long, silent moment, then he snatched the bag off the floor and sank his teeth into the vinyl.

Mama kneeled in front of him, keeping her distance, and studied him as he ate. Blood ran down his chin and soaked his already dirty shirt, droplets joining the rust-speckled ground from his previous meals.

"There has to be a way to stop this," she murmured. "But how?"

I glanced up at Christina. "Stop what?"

She shrugged, her gaze still on the black glass. "Willow. Look. Something's happening."

I leaned forward, peering back down into the

mirror. Mama's kneeling form had gone silent and pensive as she watched the vampire suck down his bag of blood. But the scene was changing. Foggy mist rolled into the bunker, though neither Mama nor the vampire seemed to notice it. The scene darkened, shadows covering Mama's face and hiding her from view. Everything went blurry until it was a melted tableau of color where nothing could be deciphered.

Then everything morphed. The bunker disappeared, replaced by open sky roiling with thunder clouds over a vast lake cradled by tall, craggy peaks. A flash of lightning illuminated the water, where rough white caps frothed angrily at the shore. Then the water breached near the shallows, and a head emerged.

A woman with turquoise hair and moonlight pale skin. She emerged from the water as dry as if it were a hot summer day. Her steps were slow and even, and the long gray cloak wrapped around her shoulders dragged through the water. Tiny sparkles of light danced around her, turning her into a beacon in the storm.

She halted on the rock bank and lifted a hand, pointing right at me. Our eyes met, and she spoke. "The Goode witch must reverse the curse before the Greene witch ends us all."

NINE

The Bloodes ate like savages then took their cheap beer to Christina's paradisiacal backyard where they made makeshift cornhole boards out of spare lumber and walnuts fresh off the tree. Once suitably gamed up, they set to work drinking one another under the table. It was like being at a Goode family reunion back in Georgia, and I would have enjoyed the bickering, laughing, and ribbing if not for the whole *we're-all-going-to-die* thing.

I made my margarita strong enough to burn my nose hairs, then settled at the kitchen island beside Dante, while Christina posted up across from us with a glass of red wine perched on her peach-painted fingertips. Sure, we were day drinking, but it seemed the best response to the creepy turquoise-haired woman who'd threatened us with extinction.

"So, by *all*," I said, tapping my fingers on my glass, "does she mean all *vampires* or the whole of the human race?"

"Or all of life as we know it," Dante added. "Like the universe might end. Finito, Milky Way."

I stared at him. "Yes, that's a nice addition to the worries I'm already harboring."

He shrugged, a sly smile touching the corners of his lips that did things to my nether regions. "Just wanted to contribute."

Christina watched the exchange with a hint of amusement, but the tiny squiggle between her brow told me she was thinking. And worrying. "Let's focus on the idea of the curse for a minute. We've discussed it as a possibility. This being, whoever she is, gave us confirmation we're correct in our assumptions regarding there being a curse on the vampires."

I shrugged. "The validation is nice, but it wasn't needed. Also, she didn't exactly say it was *just* on the vampires. She left that pretty open ended."

Christina sighed. "That is a good point. So who is she? Was the lake important to the vision? *Was* it a vision or a manifestation or a hallucination?"

"Not a hallucination," I said. "I could feel how deep her powers ran even without my own magic there to sense her. Whoever she is, she came to us on purpose specifically to give us this warning."

"To warn us of impending doom," Dante intoned.

"Not to mention," I added, giving him a pointed

look to shut up, "it seems like she was maybe monitoring for us to be looking for information on my mother. That's weird, right?"

Christina nodded. "It is."

I clutched my margarita glass tighter, a sick feeling rising in my stomach. "But I no longer have powers. So if a Goode witch is supposed to break the curse... I mean, I can't, right? I physically can't."

"You're hardly the last Goode witch," Christina pointed out. "You have a sister. Cousins. Aunts."

I rolled my eyes. "Hazel wouldn't leave Marietta even if I died. My cousins are all selfish assholes who use their magic for personal gain. They wouldn't know how to do a good deed if they were given instructions and a roadmap. The only people who might help are my great aunts, but they're so old they rode dinosaurs to church. They couldn't travel here safely."

Christina worried at her lower lip for a moment, then said, "Will, there has to be somebody. She specifically said 'the Goode witch.' We're talking about the person who needs to be around to save the world. This is big."

A pang tugged at my heart. *I* was a Goode witch once. I was a talented fire witch whose ritual magic could move mountains. For the last year, I'd managed to shove away thoughts of my powers and just *live*. I traveled instead of wallowing. I found exciting things to do, like skydiving and trekking Nepal and white water rafting through the Grand Canyon, all to keep my mind off the most important part of myself I'd lost in order to survive. But with the events of the past few days, all that avoidance had caught up to me.

I felt neutered and useless. I *wanted* to be the Goode witch meant to save the world, as Christina so eloquently put it. But I wasn't. I wasn't even a witch anymore, no matter how much I tried to pretend.

"I'll put out a call to my relatives," I said, subdued. "See if anyone bites."

"The Bloodes will help however we can," Dante offered. "They picked up a couple rooms down at The Old Circle Inn for the next couple days before they catch a plane home out of Bozeman Saturday. They'll be at our disposal."

I reached over and put my hand on his, squeezing. "That's great, Dante. Thank you." Looking back at Christina, I said, "So I'll put the feelers out for a Goode witch. We've got a Bloode gang in town. In the meantime, what's up with my mom keeping a vampire locked in a bunker?"

Dante laughed. "Yeah, what *is* up with that?"

I told them about my dad and his ridiculous need to stock up for the apocalypse, and how he'd bought the bunker off some bow hunter who owned hundreds acres of land outside the city. "I think that vision wasn't long before my parents died," I finished. "Did you see the celtic knot necklace my mother was wearing? Daddy gave that to her on their anniversary less than two months before the accident. I have it back at home in my jewelry box.”

“Do you still own the bunker?” Christina asked.

“As far as I know,” I said with a shrug. “Daddy paid cash outright for it. It would have gone to us in the trust, but you know, I bet Hazel forgot it existed after our parents died, and we went to live with Mags. I called it the castle when I was little.”

Dante pulled a fresh beer from the cardboard six pack on the counter and popped the top as he said, “So chances are the bunker has been sitting empty ever since then. Which means there could be some clues to be found regarding that vampire. Personal effects, maybe. Something.”

I raised an eyebrow. “Are you suggesting we go to Georgia?”

“That bunker is the only *real* clue we have right now,” Dante pointed out. “So we either admit defeat, or we follow the trail and hope it gives us something else to work with.”

“And if it doesn’t?” I asked.

Christina reached for the wine bottle and topped off her glass as she said, “Then we’re right back where we started. Let me tell you, my basement can’t take another demon summoning.”

The three of us laughed, and a burst of cheers and jeers in the backyard as someone missed the cornhole board lightened my spirit. For the briefest moment, we could pretend life was still normal. We were young and wild and free beneath a Montana sunset. I appreciated that.

Because I had a feeling it was all about to tumble down.

Thursday morning, I woke up as Dante feathered kisses over my stomach, then further, below my belly button, down my thigh... between my legs. Some delicious minutes later, I was *wide* awake and ready to greet the day with a satisfied smile on my face.

On the way out of town, we dropped a box of my mother's journals off to Christina so that she could get to researching while we were gone. I'd read most of them as a teen when I needed to feel close to my mother, and I didn't recall anything out of the ordinary in them, but I also hadn't been *looking* for anything back then except a tether to the woman I'd lost. Christina took the box, kissed my cheek, and told us to be careful.

Ha. As if I even knew how.

We boarded an eleven o'clock flight out of Bozeman to Atlanta, where we'd have to rent a car and drive to Marietta about thirty minutes away. Both Dante and I were what could be considered 'professional flyers' after all the traveling we'd done, both together and apart, so check in, security, and boarding went as smooth as a hot knife through real butter.

On the plane, I pulled up my texts to let Corwin know I was cutting out of town for a couple days. I didn't elaborate on what I'd been up to or any of the slim details we'd found out so far. I'd promised myself that I'd leave him alone with his grief, and I intended to keep that promise. In my empty moments, which had been notably few since Dante Bloode showed up on my doorstep, my grief crept back in like a thief to remind me that Sarah was gone forever. I felt like if I gave in to it, I'd start crying and never, ever stop.

So on the bright side, this wild goose chase was keeping me preoccupied.

When Corwin didn't reply right away, I assumed he wasn't going to reply at all and hit the back button to back out of my texts. I caught sight of Hazel's name in my inbox from the last time we'd chatted, and stared at it, conflicted.

"Do you think I should let Hazel know I'm coming?" I asked out loud. I didn't really expect Dante to have a response, but I needed to voice my worries. "Am I a bad sister if I don't?"

Dante leaned into me and nipped at my ear. "Well, you *are* a bad girl, but not a bad sister." He kissed my cheek and then pulled away, glancing out the window as the plane began to taxi. "Do you have any reason not to tell her?"

I shrugged and joined him in watching the plane move across the tarmac, gaining speed. "I guess. She doesn't know I'm a vampire. I could never... I couldn't bring myself to tell her that I lost my powers."

He reached down and squeezed my knee in solidarity.

"I haven't seen her in ages," I went on. "We're talking two years, at least. She *is* my sister, and I miss her."

"Of course you do."

I appreciated his attempts to placate me, especially since I knew that kind of thing didn't come natural to a Bloode. Even while he was trying to be supportive and make me feel better, he was still leering down the neck of my halter top. I appreciated his consistency as a person in a world full of fakes.

"But Hazel's a good egg," I said with a sigh. "She doesn't deserve the trouble I'd bring to her doorstep. She just wants to work on cars and eat junk food and drink craft beers."

"She sounds fun."

"She is." I sighed again.

Dante slid an arm around my shoulders and tugged me into his warmth. "I think the real question here is do you *really* want to involve her in this?"

I stroked the small knot of metal resting between the nodules of my collar bone. My mother's Celtic necklace, the one she'd worn in the vision we'd seen of her at Daddy's bunker. When I'd put Temperance Goode's bone necklace in my jewelry box, I'd pulled this out. "No. I don't want to disrupt her life. Hazel's not... She's kind of a quiet, reserved girl. The paranormal isn't really her thing."

"Then my vote is don't tell her," he said. "What she doesn't know can't hurt her."

But all the way through the flight, while I paged through magazines and tried to occupy my mind, I couldn't stop thinking about Hazel. If she *did* find out I was in town and hadn't told her, it *would* hurt her. So, if I wanted to fly under her radar, I needed to lay low so nobody I knew caught me. Word traveled like Goode witch fire in my hometown.

We rented a car at the Enterprise kiosk at the airport, then drove to Marietta following the GPS on Dante's phone. Once we hit familiar streets, an odd pang of homesickness hit me, and I stared silently out the window at all my old haunts.

Weird, going home after so many years away. I'd cut out of Marietta not long after my seventeenth birthday, and I hadn't come back. The one time I'd seen Hazel since, we'd met in Atlanta while I was on layover heading somewhere else. This was my home. This was where I learned magic, where I figured out who I was and what I wanted out of life. Where I decided what I wanted was to get the hell out of my hometown the minute I had my diploma in hand.

It looked different now, on the other side of undeath. More lively, more vibrant, more beautiful. Maybe absence really did make the heart grow fonder.

Once we hit the outskirts of town, I took over

giving directions, surprised that I still knew where the hell I was going. We left the main road for a small side road, and then left *that* road for a narrow dirt lane hardly big enough for the rental coupe. The sun was fading in a big red sky as Dante pulled up outside the bunker entrance and cut the engine.

Weeds and ivy had grown so heavy around the structure that the door was no longer visible. It looked like a tall, misshapen hill in desperate need of a weed whacker. Unfortunately, we hadn't packed that in our carry-ons, so any weed whacking we did would have to be with our bare hands.

We got out and worked on clearing the heavy over-growth so we could reach the entrance, both of us cussing and grunting as we caught our fingers on brambles. It took muscles I didn't know I had to leverage the largest, most tenacious of the weeds out of the ground. As we worked, the sun crept closer to the horizon, and the clearing began to fall into purple twilight. The idea of getting caught out here in the dark made me shiver, though I didn't know why. Maybe because I could feel the memories on the air, sense my parents' ghosts with the veil between the worlds so thin.

Once the door was visible, Dante grabbed the handle and tried to open it. "Locked. Ow." He let go of the handle quickly, sucking in a hiss of pain. "And warded, too."

"Like with magic?" I asked.

Dante raised an eyebrow. "What other kind of ward would there be, Will?"

I nodded. "Good point. Can you break it?"

Dante ran his hands over the weathered wood door. The red paint had long since faded to a dusty peach. "It's strong. Your mom was one badass witch, wasn't she?"

"She was. My Aunt Mags used to call me Laurel by accident. She said I not only look just like my mama, but I practice magic like her, too."

"Well, then you're a little too good," Dante remarked and stepped away from the door. "Because this ward is blood magic, and if we try to break through it, it'll kill us both."

TEN

I paced back and forth in front of the bunker, considering our options.

Blood magic was one of the most potent forms of raw energy. Blood rituals were almost always destructive in nature—even the good ones—because no witch could truly control a blood ritual. Using blood in magic made it volatile, almost like it gave the magic a mind of its own. Even Dante and his Bloode family were at the mercy of botched spells with more power than any one man could handle. Though, to be fair, since they were spirit witches, they were also neatly posed to have better control than most.

"How do we break through the ward?" I murmured under my breath, pausing long enough to glare at the door before I resumed my trek. "I didn't even know Mama knew how to do blood rituals. Why on earth did she ward the door?"

"My guess is she warded it to keep the vampire in," Dante offered. He'd sat down on the pad of concrete in front of the door and leaned back against the exposed earth. The setting sun cast his face in shadow, so that the hard angles of his face stood out in sharp relief. He looked like some kind of earth spirit. Or a demon about to ask for my soul.

Sorry, I already gave it up, I thought jokingly. There was a lot more I'd give him, though, if he asked. More than I ever thought possible.

I paused in front of him. "You're right. She warded it in case he broke his chains. Yeah, I guess that makes sense. But the door's been warded all this time? Fuck..." I glanced past him at the weathered wood, as if it would give me answers. "Dante, you don't think he's still down there, do you?"

He shook his head. "No way. It's been what, a decade since your parents died?"

"Longer," I murmured. I didn't like to think about it.

"Without access to blood, he would have withered away and died. No vampire could survive that long without food. If anything, we'll go down there and find his corpse."

I shuddered. "I hope, for his sake and ours, that my mother dealt with him before she died. Okay," I said, resuming my pacing, "the wards. Chances are, just from knowing how Aunt Mags operated, Mama would have set this up so that the family could get in.

Meaning me, Hazel, Mags… And you're sure it's blood magic?"

He held up three fingers, pressed together. "Scout's honor. Never been a scout, but I've got honor. And that ward tastes like blood."

"So it stands to reason that's Mama's blood," I mused. "Goode witch blood. My blood may be as dried up as old prunes, but it's still Goode blood, right?"

Dante laughed. "Interesting visual, but yes. Your blood, even when dried up like an old prune, is still Goode witch blood for the purposes of magic."

I halted my pacing again and wrapped my around my chest. "I'm not a witch anymore. So it's just Goode blood."

"Doesn't matter," Dante said firmly. "Blood is blood. You having powers or not having powers has no bearing on the potency. Just like the fact it's pruny old vampire blood won't change anything, either."

I grinned. "You might be my favorite human ever. Don't tell Christina."

Dante zipped his lips. "Your secret dies with me."

Resuming my pacing, I went on. "I've got the blood but not the magic words," I said as my feet sank into the soft dirt. Night was falling so swiftly that my feet disappeared in the dark grass. "I was never here with her after she brought the vampire home; I think I'd remember that. So I don't even have memories to go on of how she got in."

"What if…" Dante climbed to his feet nimbly and

joined me on the grass. He lassoed me around the waist and pulled me to a halt beside him, both of us facing the bunker. "What if you bleed for the door, and I'll try a basic unwarding."

"You said it could kill us."

"No, I said trying to break through the door without breaking the ward would kill us," he corrected. "I don't know for certain that attempting to drop the ward will kill us."

"What percentage of uncertainty are we talking here?" I said wryly.

"Five percent. Give or take how devious your mother was."

"I mean, she was harboring a vampire in my daddy's apocalypse bunker. Clearly, I didn't know her as well as I thought I did."

Dante nudged me with an elbow. "You were just a kid. I'm a grown ass man, and still can't get my dad to confide in me."

I nodded, though it still hurt. Laurel Goode had way more layers than I ever imagined, and I couldn't even peel them away to discover more about her because she was gone.

Life was so unfair.

"Do you have a knife?" I asked, holding out a hand.

Dante reached into his front pocket and extracted a switchblade—the super illegal kind. I raised an eyebrow as the blade *snick*ed out of its sheath with sharp, deadly force, but I took it from him anyway.

"Dante Bloode, you rebel," I said. "It's a federal crime to buy, possess, or carry a switchblade."

"I march to the beat of my own laws," he quipped. "When did you get your Supreme Court Judge appointment?"

I laughed and positioned the knife over my hand.

He reached out and caught my wrist before I could slice the blade across my palm, and I glanced up, startled by his sudden movement. He tugged me into him so hard I basically stumbled into his embrace, and if it weren't for his grasp on my wrist, I'd probably have skewered him with the knife. Then his lips were on mine, and I wasn't so worried about warded doors, illegal knives, and vampire corpses.

Dante's kiss was hot in more ways than one. He fisted a palmful of my ass and yanked me tighter to his body as the kiss deepened. Our tongues mingled, bringing to mind every night I'd ever spent in his arms, our bodies entwined. I wanted to spend the rest of my life tasting his lips.

I'd never wanted "the rest of my life" before, and the thought terrified me. Especially with a guy like Dante Bloode. This little adventure we'd shared had shown me that he felt real affection for me, but I couldn't imagine he'd ever be the "rest of my life" kind of guy.

He finally pulled away enough to smile down at me. We were both breathing hard, and I'd given more than a little thought to undressing him here and now and fucking on the dirt outside the bunker. I mean, hey, there was no one around.

"Just in case we do die," Dante told me, squeezing my ass one more time before he released me. "I wanna go out thinking dirty thoughts of you."

"Pig," I said, and then kissed him one more time, for good measure.

The knife bit into my palm with a sharp sting, and I gave my fist a couple of squeezes to get my dead blood moving. Maroon liquid oozed out the gash slowly, until my skin was stained like I'd spilled red wine. Then I pressed my palm to the bunker door and looked expectantly at Dante.

He stepped up behind me and grasped my shoulder with one hand, then put his palm on the door beside mine. Once the circle was complete, he spoke a short phrase in Latin that, of course, I didn't understand.

I waited breathlessly, watching his face. A split second later, he grinned and pulled his hand away from the wood as he glanced down at me. "Unwarded."

"You're a genius," I told him, wiping my palm on my blue jeans. You didn't become a vampire without learning how to get blood out of clothing, so I'd deal with it later. "You know, Goode witches just use English. This is America. And Latin's been dead since, like, Roman times or something."

Dante slapped my butt. "So much snark." He

reached past me for the door handle and gave it a jiggle. "Still locked though."

"I figured. Let the vampire work." I waved my hand to indicate he should step away. Then I took the handle in hand, gave a good, strong, vampire-driven jerk, and pulled the whole damn thing right off.

"See." I shoved the broken door inward on horror-movie hinges. "All better."

"I think the words you're looking for are all broken," Dante said dryly, but he preceded me into the darkness, turning on the flashlight on his phone to light the way.

As Dante headed down the stairs with his dinky light, I tried the switch at the top, but nothing happened. The generator probably ran out of juice ages ago. I didn't fancy going down into the dark, dank hole with nothing but the LED on his phone, but we didn't have much choice unless we wanted to detour to Walmart for bigger flashlights.

Time already felt like a ticking bomb about to drop, so that wasn't an option.

"Smells like mold," Dante remarked as we stepped off the last stair together. "I'd diagnose water damage."

"I'm not looking to buy or sell," I told him, amused.

We ventured further into the room with Dante's phone lighting the way. Everything looked as I remembered it, though covered in an inch of dust. The shelves loomed like mountains in the small circle of light, more than six feet tall and piled with canned goods and other necessities. One shelving unit held all toilet paper, and another held a bunch of air-tight canisters that my memories told me held sugar and flour. I'd helped open bags and transfer the contents under my father's watchful eye.

I traced my fingers over the things I passed, feeling closer to Daddy than I'd felt in a long time. Mama had made fun of him mercilessly for this bunker, but she'd loved him so much, she would have let him do anything if his heart desired it. My fingers came away coated in thick dust that felt like velvet, and it reminded me how dusty my memories had become. But walking these narrow aisles, seeing these things that I'd watched Daddy place on these shelves with his strong, sure hands… It felt like walking through a living memory.

"You could ride out an actual apocalypse in here," Dante said, picking up a box of ammunition. "Guns, food, water, toiletries. A nuke could wipe out half the eastern seaboard, and this would be the new nirvana."

"That was the plan," I said, glancing at the row of guns on the shelf next to him.

"Did he actually think an apocalypse was pending?"

I laughed. "There's always an apocalypse pending somewhere. It's all a matter of which way the cat jumps."

At the end of the aisle, I stepped out into the larger area of concrete where Daddy had fashioned a living space. I remembered the tiny kitchenette in the corner that Mama had complained would *never* be big enough for a southern woman. A narrow, folding door beside that covered the tiny bathroom, complete with a working septic tank, while a small kitchen table sat nearby. A second hand couch and loveseat were situated around a wide, 70s-fabulous coffee table, and in the other corner, the bunk beds.

Two sets of metal bunks were built right into the wall of the bunker. I'd loved them when I was little—climbing inside one was like taking solitude in my own little fortress. I used to beg Mama to let me and Hazel have a sleepover here, and she never would.

The beds weren't exactly in the same shape they'd been twelve years ago. All four mattresses had been pulled out of the cubbies and lay in fluffy pieces around the concrete. Blankets had been ripped to shreds, tatters scattered around the floor. Everything around the sleeping area had been destroyed until it looked like a battleground.

And a form lay on the solid wood planks of a bottom bunk.

Ew, the body, I thought as we walked closer. It had occurred to me that Mom's death would have left the vampire here to die, if she hadn't released him from his misery beforehand, but the proof of it was hard to swallow.

We gazed down at the creature, and Dante made a sound of pity. "Wow. Looks like a mummy."

And he did. His skin had grown dry, papery brown, and clung to his bones until he looked like a preserved corpse. His clothes were even dirtier than he'd been in the vision, and his hair hung in tangles past his shoulders. A bushy brown beard hung down his chest. How fast did beards grow? How long had he been locked in here before he died?

"Poor guy. Mom died, and he never stood a chance," I murmured.

Then the corpse opened his eyes, let out a shrill screech, and lunged for Dante.

CHAPTER

ELEVEN

I reacted out of sheer reflex.

My fist caught the vampire on the side of his face with a bone-crunching jolt. He let out a pained grunt and sailed sideways, collapsing over the side of the bunk bed in a broken heap on the floor.

"Run!" I shouted to Dante, giving him a shove towards the front of the bunker.

We took off, fear and adrenaline sending us reeling through the shelving units, knocking things off shelves in our haste to get away from the crazed vampire. I managed to keep enough presence of mind to snag a shotgun off the shelf as we passed the cache of guns, and then nabbed a box of ammunition to boot, hoping like hell Dante knew how to load the damn thing, because I sure didn't.

We sailed up the narrow stairway and back out into the evening. I slammed the door shut behind us and leaned against it while I held out the shotgun and box of ammunition. "Can you work this thing?"

Dante took the gun and ammo and set to work loading shells with a speed and efficiency that told me he did, in fact, have extensive experience with shotguns. The way his long fingers worked the weapon over made me wish *I* was a gun.

"How the hell is he still alive?" I asked, my voice faintly breathless from our flight.

"I wouldn't have considered it possible," Dante replied, his own tone much more calm and even than mine. He set the barrel of the gun on his shoulder and regarded me. "You holding up the door for any particular reason?"

"I'm hoping he isn't strong enough to break past me!" I snapped. "There's no doorknob!"

Dante chuckled. "He's chained to the bunk bed. Did you not see it?"

"Oh. No." I straightened and wobbled a little bit on my shaky knees. I had no doubts that I could take that creature on and come out the victor, if it came down to it, but the jump scare of expecting a corpse and getting a blood-lust ravenous monster instead would have stopped my heart, if it weren't already dead. "Okay, so we can safely go back down there. Armed," I added, motioning to the gun. "I'm going to call Corwin for help."

I retrieved my cell phone from my purse on the floorboard of the rental, then scrolled until I found

Corwin's name. I didn't have to scroll far—my circle was so small now, it was barely a triangle. Christina, Dante, and Corwin.

"Pick up, pick up, pick up," I chanted as I listened to the line ring. I knew without really knowing that he hadn't left his house in days. I also knew he was probably cooped up in his bedroom with a cooler of bagged blood and the entire Audrey Hepburn oeuvre on remastered DVD. When he didn't answer the first time, I called back. When he didn't answer the second time, I texted *911!!!!!!!!!!* And then called again.

This time, he answered.

"Are you all right?" Corwin said shortly. "I'm busy."

"Sucking down O-Neg while watching *Roman Holiday* isn't busy," I snapped back. "It's wallowing. Meanwhile, I'm at a secret apocalypse bunker with a vampire who hasn't had blood in a decade. You wanna help me out or nah?"

There was a beat of perplexed silence, and then Corwin said, "Please start at the beginning and leave nothing out."

So I spent several moments catching Corwin up to speed on everything that had happened since he drove away in his sleek little Audi the day after Sarah's funeral. By the time I'd laid out the whole sordid tale, beginning to end, I could almost hear his anxiety bubbling over the phone line.

"Clearly, I should never leave you to your own devices," Corwin said. "Perhaps this is my fault."

"Stop with the martyr act," I said irritably, my gaze searching out Dante in the ever-growing shadows. He was nothing but a shadow himself as he walked around the bunker, gun held at the ready. "I'm pursuing this investigation because I want to, not because you twisted my arm. You haven't even been in contact enough to hug me, much less twist anything."

Corwin sighed. "I'm sorry, Willow. I've let my emotions get the better of me."

"Yeah, well, I guess you have a right to that. But while you're hanging out in the deep end of your whole grieving, woe-is-me pool, could you maybe throw me a life raft?"

"What do you need to know?"

Dante stopped and whipped around, pulling the gun up like a soldier in combat. I rolled my eyes and turned my back on his antics. "How long can a vampire exist without blood?"

Corwin blew out a breath - an old human habit, since he didn't need to breathe. "Oh, I don't know. I suppose indefinitely, but I can't say I've ever known anyone who's gone without to have any kind of base-line. I would imagine after so long, the body would go into a kind of suspended animation."

"Suspended animation suddenly reanimated by the smell of human blood?" I asked.

"I suppose," Corwin agreed.

"The dude's crazed. He tried to bite Dante, and there was *nothing* human in his eyes. Can he even be brought back from that?"

"There's no way to know, but to try," Corwin said simply. "I'd suggest human blood. Fresh would likely be preferable, but I'd assume he's in such a state that he'd maul the donor to death. So bagged blood, maybe a dozen sacks. Offer them to him slowly. Too much, too fast could send him into blood shock."

"Got it." I cringed. "You don't by chance have a bagged blood contact in Marietta?"

"Call Hooper, Weaver & Sons," he instructed me. "Tell them to put it on my bill. And Willow?"

"Hmm?"

"Don't get your hopes up," Corwin warned. "After so many years without sustenance, there is a possibility this man will be beyond redemption."

I nodded, even though he couldn't see me. "Yeah. Thanks, Corwin. Thanks for picking up the phone."

"I apologize for not doing so the first time. Be safe, and let me know what happens."

I ended the call and shoved my cell in my back pocket, then turned to Dante. He was still stalking around the tall grass behind the bunker, pointing the gun at imaginary creatures like he was Elmer-damn-Fudd.

"We need blood," I called to him, cringing as something crashed deep beneath the bunker on the other side of the door. "A *lot* of blood."

TURNED OUT, Hooper, Weaver & Sons had branches all over the continental United States, and within the hour, we were loaded down with two styrofoam coolers equipped with ice packs and twelve vinyl sacks of fresh human blood. I didn't know whether to continue being impressed by how quickly and easily they could fix a vampire's little "problems," or to be totally, thoroughly wigged out by it.

Dante carried the coolers while I hefted the shotgun and took the lead down the bunker stairs. Chain or no chain, I didn't want to risk the vampire having a clear shot at Dante's delicious red wine veins. I'd never been really great at sharing, so the lunatic vamp was going to get a slug in the head before he could get his hands on my man.

I eased down the aisle, my gaze everywhere all at once and my vampire senses on high alert. I heard rustling from the back of the room, and the scraping clink of chain on stone. Then we left the shelves behind for the living area

The vampire stood in front of the bunk beds, shoulders hunched and drool hanging in strings from his dry, cracked lips. At the sound of our footfalls on the dusty floor, he whirled around and hissed at us like a feral cat. He raised both hands in a fair imitation of claws - especially since his fingernails were long and sharp. He blinked into Dante's flashlight as if it burned his eyes.

"Dante, give me a bag," I said softly, keeping my gaze, and the gun, on the vampire. I maneuvered a hand free and held it out, palm up, until I felt the cold weight of the bag press down against my skin.

The vampire continued to hiss and snarl, tugging at the end of his chain so violently I could see skin flaying around his wrists. His dark eyes were unfocused, and his nostrils flared, either from fear or the scent of Dante's blood singing through his veins. But I kept my own body firmly between the vamp and my boyfriend, because if those chains broke, I'd kill the monster without a second thought.

But first, I wanted to give him a chance to drink, and a chance to see if the crazed demeanor faded after a few bags.

I tossed the first one across the few feet separating us. It rolled gushily over the concrete and came to rest at the vampire's dirty bare feet. For a moment, I thought he was too far gone to even recognize what it was. But then his nostrils flared and his pupils dilated until his eyes were nothing but black and white. He fell on the bag and tore into it with his teeth.

Half the blood ended up down his front in the midst of his fervor. He drained what was left, and then lifted the front of his T-shirt to lick at what had spilled. I raised an eyebrow, grossed out, then got distracted by a tap at my shoulder as Dante offered me a second bag of blood.

Corwin had said to go slow, but the poor thing had spilled half the first bag. So I tossed him another.

This time, the vampire was more careful. He sank his fangs into the plastic without ripping them out and he slurped at the blood like a kid with a Capri Sun. As he drank, his gaze roamed over me and Dante with a little more recognition, though that crazy look never fell from his face.

My arms were straining from the uncomfortable position of holding the gun, but I didn't drop the barrel. I waited five minutes after he drained the second bag, while he licked and sucked at his fingers, arms, and clothes, then gave him a third.

Patience had never been one of my virtues, but I did my best to channel Corwin's stalwart nature as I waited ten minutes before passing the fourth bag over. In the interim, the vampire stood over the mess of blood and emptied bags, his fists clenching and unclenching, and his gaze faraway, as if his mind were trying to make a comeback. He only stirred when the fourth bag hit his toes.

We went on like this for the next thirty minutes. With every bag, the vampire breathed a little slower, stood a little taller. His skin started to look less like paper and turned rounder, plumper, a little pinker. By the tenth bag, a hint of humanity had returned to his eyes, and with it, wariness.

With the eleventh bag in hand, he backed into the space between the bunk beds, where my father had built in a set of dresser drawers, and stared at us. He gripped the blood bag between both hands, taking intermittent sips as he watched us.

Then he spoke. His voice was as dry as an autumn leaf scraping against the sidewalk, and he stumbled over each word as if he'd forgotten how to form the sounds with his lips. "When... i-is it?"

"Twenty-thirteen," I said gently, lowering the barrel on the gun. "A few days before Halloween."

The vampire slumped against the wall, clutching the bag against his bloodied chest. His eyelids drooped shut. "Lord h-help me."

"When were you brought here?"

He blinked at me, and I could almost see the gears turning in his head. "Ninety-six. J-just after the s-shiny ball."

"Shiny ball?"

He sank his teeth into the bag again and ignored me so thoroughly, it was as if I hadn't spoken at all. One second, he was there, lucid; the next second, gone.

I glanced back at Dante to see if he had any insight. His dark eyes were narrowed and his face thoughtful as he attempted to puzzle out the answer.

"The new year," he said after a moment. "When the shiny ball drops."

Horror washed over me. The man had been in this bunker for almost eighteen years.

Something changed in the vampire's face then, and he snarled and lunged for us. Luckily, the chains held, but I whipped up the shotgun, just in case.

"She promised to take care of me!" he roared, pulling so hard against his manacles that his body leaned forward and dangled like an arrow pointing toward me. "She fed me and then she... didn't. Stop. Alone." He howled and fell to his knees, spreading the congealing leftovers of his dinner over the dusty floor.

All the wind left my sails. I lowered the gun and turned to look at Dante. "He's too far gone. There's no way he can tell us anything about my mother."

"Laurel," the vampire rasped.

I whipped around, shocked to hear Mama's name. "Yes, Laurel. That's my mother."

"Y-you look like h-her." He dangled against his chains, his forehead pressed against one taut arm. "She saved me from the demon inside me. For a time. He's back. Can never get away."

"What demon?" I hoped he'd retain some of that lucidity enough to give me answers.

"Vampire." He closed his eyes. "Half but also human. I lost the human."

I took a step forward in my shock and lowered the gun. There was *no* way I'd heard his mad hatter nonsense right. "Are you telling me you're half-vampire, half-human?"

He snorted, and a crazed grin painted across his face. "Half and half. Like for coffee. I miss coffee."

"Hey, no, rein in the crazy, Loony Tunes," I snapped. "What did Laurel want with you?"

His grin sank away. "I murder. Laurel saved me. Said I could save her world."

"Save her world? Save *the* world?" I clarified.

The vampire shrugged. "The prey does not confide in the predator."

I groaned and turned away from him before I did something stupid like punch him for his Confuscianisms. Grabbing the last bag of blood from the cooler, I threw it to him underhand, then left him to his feast.

"Mama knew something," I told Dante. "Something important to saving the world. Something to do with him." I hooked a thumb over my shoulder to indicate the vampire.

The vampire's voice floated back to me, thick with blood. "Mama knew a lot of things."

Sighing, I turned back to the madman. "What's that supposed to mean?"

"Prophecy." Blood spittle poured over his lips, and he paused, tongue darting between his two sharp canines to clean the mess. His entire beard glistened darkly red. "The gift of foresight."

"Mama didn't have the gift of foresight."

"She did." He nodded vehemently, beard bobbing, eyes alight with madness. "Visions. Lakes. Zombies. Half-vampire, half-human, save her world." The vampire tossed the final empty blood bag to the floor. "Only a Goode witch."

I ignored that stupid phrase I was getting tired of hearing and zeroed in on the one word he'd said that had pinged my radar. "Lakes?"

"One lake to save us all." He cackled, long and loud. Then his face changed again. Such a subtle difference - a tightening of his lips, narrowing eyes, flaring nostrils like a bull ready to charge. Seventeen years of isolation was enough to break a man, and all the blood bags in the world couldn't bring back whoever he was before.

But when he charged this time, the two decades-old chains finally gave out.

TWELVE

Even after an hour-long shower in the hotel's fancy tub, I could still feel that poor vampire's blood on my skin as I dried off next to the foggy mirror and listened to the last of the water draining in the silence.

I'd shot without even giving him a chance, and it weighed on me. Heavily. Stranger or not, he and I were the same. Well, close to the same, if his half-human, half-vampire nature had been true. All I could see was the fear on Dante's face, and I knew he wouldn't be strong enough to fight off the vampire.

We were too quick. Too strong. I liked teasing him during foreplay and holding him down so that he couldn't move. He got off on it, the whole "big, bad vampire" routine, especially when I was doing dirty things to him at the same time.

But this situation hadn't been sexy, and Dante

alive was much more preferable than Dante dead. Add the strange vampire's madness on top of his preternatural abilities, and Dante was a dead man.

So I'd taken the guy's head off with the shotgun. Literally. A point blank round right between his eyes, and his head exploded like a watermelon dropped from a four-storey window. Even vampires couldn't come back from that.

We left a hell of a mess on my daddy's bunker floor. I never wanted to go back there again. All my mother's secrets were encapsulated in that underground hole.

I wrapped my dark hair in a towel and tugged on one of the hotel's fluffy white robes, then left the steam of the bathroom for the cool AC of the bedroom.

Dante sat up against the headboard, his laptop open on his thighs and his legs stretched out across the blankets, ankles crossed. He'd showered first, in and out, because he knew I wanted a chance to stand beneath the water for a hundred years, and his normally pompadour'd hair lay flat against his head. It made him look less like a Disney villain and more like... my boyfriend.

He glanced up from the screen and leered at me. "You naked under there?"

"No, I'm wearing a parka and long johns," I shot back, rolling my eyes.

He winked at me, then turned back to his

computer screen. "Christina called your cell while you were in the shower."

"I'm surprised she's up this late. I need to talk to her anyway." I crossed to the dresser, the industrial carpet rough on my bare feet. Sure enough, my phone showed a missed call from Christina Steele. I pulled up the log and called back.

She answered on the first ring. "Hey, how'd the search of the bunker go?"

"Not exactly as planned," I said as I dropped into the armchair next to the television. I told her about the vampire and everything that had happened, and she listened in rapt silence. "So we really didn't find out anything that can help us. My mom was keeping a half-vampire, half-human prisoner because he could save the world. She had the gift of foresight, and knew something about zombies, a lake, and the end of the world. A bunch more questions without any answers. And me over here wondering why the fuck she never mentioned any of this to Hazel or me."

"A lake," Christina mused. "Like the lake in the vision. Will, I *did* find mention of a lake in your mother's journals. I can't remember... let me find the passage. I'm pretty sure I marked it."

The sound of pages feathering crossed the phone line. I crossed my legs and leaned back against the cushioned seat, glancing at the clock on the table beside me. Already close to midnight. I couldn't wait to crawl in bed and pass out. Although, the way Dante was eyeing my bare thigh where the robe had fallen away, I had a feeling I'd be getting a workout before that could happen.

Christina came back over the line. "Okay, yes, I found it. She wrote of a lake that can 'neutralize any curse or negative energy.' She also wrote that it's heavily guarded, and 'Only a Goode witch' can find it."

"Great, another reminder that I'm no longer a Goode witch." I sighed and glanced at Dante. He was dividing his attention between his computer screen and my bare legs. If I raised one off the cushion, I was ninety percent positive his gaze would follow it, like a cat following a fly. "But there's a Goode witch right here in Marietta. I really don't want to involve my sister in this, though. Do we have any other options?"

Christina hummed, then said, "Just get a vial of her blood. We don't even need much."

"And how do you propose I get a vial of Hazel's blood without her knowing about it?"

She paused for a moment, then offered, "What about a sleep spell?"

"A sleep spell," I repeated, looking pointedly at Dante. "Can you do that?"

"A toddler can do that," he replied without looking away from the glow of his screen.

"My toddler can do that," I told Christina, earning a laugh.

"Good. Get the blood, then get back home. I'll have everything ready for the spell when you get here."

We said our goodbyes, and I hung up, feeling forlorn that I couldn't just set my phone down, crawl beneath the sheets, and pass out. Now, we had to go break into my sister's house and somehow obtain a vial of her blood without her knowledge.

But first...

Dante closed his laptop, his gaze raking over me. "Do we have time—"

I untied the belt and let my robe fall off my shoulders. "We always have time for that."

WITH MY BODY—AND my blood lust—appeased, I dressed in all black like a ninja, and then Dante drove us across town to my sister's apartment.

Since moving out of Aunt Mags' house, Hazel had been sharing a place with a roommate, someone she'd found in the classifieds. The arrangement seemed to work out, since Hazel worked most of the day doing oil changes at Valvoline, and her roommate worked nights at Wal-Mart, stocking. Hazel had told me it meant that most days, she felt like she lived alone. Which meant good news for us, since Hazel would be sound asleep at this time of night, and her roommate hopefully wouldn't be home.

Dante parked two blocks down on the street, and we walked the rest of the way to the strip of town-homes. The building was a flat-fronted red brick row segmented into two-storey apartments, each with an identical blue door. Hazel's bicycle was chained to the iron railing next to the two shallow stone steps leading to her door, but the two parking spaces directly in front of her place were empty. Bingo—roommate was at work.

Being the jet-setting baby sister, I had a key to Hazel's place on the off chance I might ever need to come "home." We let ourselves in as silently as possible, slipping into the pitch dark foyer with as much care as if the floor were made of shattered glass.

After I closed the door, I stood, fingers still resting on the doorknob as I listened to the apartment. My vampire senses found one person in occupancy—Hazel, snoring lightly, her body temperature on the low end to indicate that she'd already reached her REM cycle.

I motioned for Dante to follow me down the hallway. The place was sparse but clean—no artwork, photos, or prints on the white walls, but the hardwood floors were speckled with colorful rugs. We passed an immaculate living room with only a couch and a television on a folding card table, and beyond that, a dark windowless bathroom. A jacket hung on the bottom railing, and I recognized the corduroy and hooded sweatshirt combination of Hazel's jacket. I paused to press my face to the soft green fabric and breathed in her scent. Rose oil, a habit she picked up from Aunt Mags, and an undercurrent of motor oil.

I stood there for several seconds, clinging to Hazel's jacket, to the scent of her and the memories that came with it. Long summers at Aunt Mags' homestead. Puzzles on the screened porch, and building a fort in our bedroom from blankets and pillows. This time of year, we would have been watching every Halloween and horror movie that existed, eating mini Snickers and sneaking Cokes in from the 7-11, since Aunt Mags refused to have soda in the house.

A wave of grief powered through me, and I dropped her jacket back onto the railing. "Come on," I said to Dante, as if I weren't the one who'd held us up.

Hazel's bedroom door was closed, but not locked, and I took my time turning the knob and sliding into the cool, dim interior. I listened to her breathing the entire time to make sure nothing changed, but she was out cold. So much so, that we both sidled up to the edge of her bed in breathless silence.

Dante was nothing but a shadow in the dark as he held his hands out over Hazel's sleeping body. For the nine hundredth time in the past few days, I wished I could feel the wash of his magic rolling over Hazel, over me, over the room. I absolutely *lusted* for the feeling, like a junkie craving a hit. But I had to wait for him to cast the sleep spell, then let me know it was in operation.

If it weren't for my vampire night sight, I wouldn't have been able to see his grin in the dark room as he motioned for me to get to work.

My sluggish, undead heart made an effort to beat a little faster in anticipation. I just knew as soon as the needle punctured her skin, she'd wake up. I'd have a hell of a lot of explaining to do if that happened.

I carefully pulled her arm out from beneath the covers, sparing a glance for her sleeping face. My sister was beautiful - the kind of beautiful that came effortlessly. Golden hair, pale skin, almost six feet tall with a strong, lithe body that always held a little extra curve. She didn't need make up or fancy clothes. Hazel was just as beautiful in her Valvoline uniform as she was in jeans and a T-shirt.

Even while she slept, I felt short, dumpy, and very, very different from her with my long dark hair and naturally tanned complexion. I looked like our mother; Mama always said Hazel had taken after her biological father, who neither of us had ever known.

I rolled her arm over. She had bruises up and down her skin, though that wasn't abnormal since she worked with her hands, elbow-deep in machinery. I kept one eye on her face and the other on her arteries as I tied a length of twine around her bicep to make her veins bulge.

"Do I want to know why you know how to do this?" Dante whispered.

"Some people don't like to be bitten," I replied, uncapping the needle.

He pouted. "You bite other people?"

"You want me to starve when I'm not around you?" I hissed.

Dante stepped closer to me, his lips hovering near my ear. "What would you think about making this a permanent thing?"

I froze, the sharp needle less than an inch from Hazel's skin. His lips wrapped around my earlobe, and he took hold of my hips with both hands.

"You and me," he said, the words nothing but a breath.

"This is a really bad time for this conversation."

"I could move to Shadow Hollow," he went on, his fingers tightening on my hips. "I can work for my dad from anywhere."

I pulled back from Hazel's arm and whirled on him. "Is this a territorial thing?"

He looked taken aback, and his hands fell away from my body. "What?"

"First, you didn't like the charade I played with Hank the serial cannibal, and now you're proposing a relationship because I bite other people. So do you *really* want to be with me, or are you just, like, a pitbull pissing on his tree?"

We stared at each other in charged silence for several long seconds, and then both started laughing at the same time—doing our damnedest to keep it quiet. Sleep spell or not, I didn't want to risk my sister waking up.

"If you're serious," I added, "we can talk about this when I'm not about to stab my sister. Okay?"

He nodded. "Yeah. Stab away."

I gave him one more look, reeling from the conversation, and turned back to Hazel's veins.

My sister had great blood pressure. Usually, the minute the red liquid began to flow into the vial, I'd salivate like someone had put a big juicy steak in front of me. But Goode witch blood was *my* blood; it was my past, present, and future, everything that shaped me and formed who I became. The vampire could take my magic, but it couldn't take my blood. So rather than seeing it whoosh into the vial like filet mignon, I saw it drain from my sister and connect us on a soul-deep, fundamental level that nothing else could.

I wished I could wake her up, wrap her in a hug, and tell her I loved her.

But I just finished filling the vial, removed the IV needle, and put the whole lot of it in the tiny satchel hanging around my neck.

"Got what we need?" Dante asked softly.

"Yeah. Let's bounce." I took hold of his arm and started to pivot away from Hazel's bed.

Then my sister sat straight up, looked around the room, and barked, "Who's there?"

THIRTEEN

I froze like a deer in headlights, my fingers still clutching Dante's sleeve.

There was movement from Hazel's bed, and then a flame flared to life, hovering gracefully over my sister's palm. Orange light illuminated her face, casting her features into deep shadow. Her thick, gold hair was pulled into a low braid, and the flame morphed her brown eyes to deep amber. We looked nothing alike - Hazel tall and muscular, me short and curvy, her skin pale like moonlight, mine two shades lighter than my Native American grandmother's on my father's side.

But there she was. My sister. The girl who'd been my whole world for most of my life.

I felt a pang deep, down inside to see her, so close and so familiar.

"Show yourself!" Hazel snapped, glaring around

the dark room. The warm molasses drawl of her voice, coupled with her anger, sent a wave of pre-teen angst through me. She'd used that voice on me more than a few times when I acted up. She never missed anything I did.

Except for now. We were *right there.* Right in front of her. Yet her shrewd gaze swept past us twice without any indication that she could see or sense us.

Dante tugged against my grip on his arm, drawing my attention silently. I glanced at him, and he placed a finger to his lips. Hazel's flame glittered off his cerulean eyes, and one corner of his lips tilted up sardonically, making him look like a chiseled hunk of demon luring me to hell. He motioned with his head for me to back away.

He'd spelled us. A glamour, maybe, or a veil to camouflage us. Something that kept Hazel from being able to see us. Clever, clever hottie.

Hazel flipped her blankets aside with her free hand and put her feet to the floor. "I know you're there!"

We moved faster, backing away from her as she stood up. Luckily, we'd left the door to her bedroom open when we came in, which she was sure to notice, but at least it meant a quick getaway.

Hazel lifted her hand to hold the fire out ahead of her, but halted with a grimace. "Ow. What the..." She glanced down to inspect the inside of her elbow where I'd drawn her blood.

Time to go. I yanked Dante after me and fled the

house before my sister could figure out there was a teeny tiny hole in her arm.

ON THE BRIGHT SIDE, TSA didn't seem to notice anything weird about the decorative, Victorian-era necklace I wore when I passed through security at the airport the next morning. Good thing, too, since the ornate metal vial held my sister's blood, and I was pretty sure blood on a plane fell under "items not allowed."

I buzzed with unrestrained energy the entire flight home, driving Dante so crazy that I considered asking him if he'd rethought his whole "let's make this permanent" thing. But I didn't actually want to know the answer to that question.

I'd never wanted permanent. I'd never wanted more than a weekend, really. But all the time we'd spent together before, all the memories we'd made together, when I added them all up, Dante was exactly the kind of man I could see myself with indefinitely. He had the same sense of adventure, and the same disregard for what was *right* versus what was *fun but doesn't hurt anybody, so what's the harm?*

And I liked being around him. I liked the way he hooked his fingers into my belt loops when he talked to me. I liked the way he called me "babe" and sucked his teeth when he was thinking *really* hard. I liked his stupid haircut with its gelled poof and the way his undercut felt like velvet on my fingertips and the way his body fit perfectly against mine.

If there was a forever, maybe it could be with Dante.

But I didn't say any of that because I was a fucking coward. Instead, I restlessly paged through every magazine I'd brought with me, stared out the window, and fretted about whether or not Hazel's blood would work without all the rest of her there, too.

When our plane touched down in Bozeman and I turned my phone on, I found a text from my sister waiting for me.

Weirdest dream last night! I could have sworn you were here. Miss you.

She didn't mention doors that shouldn't have been open or a tiny hole in her arm surrounded by strange bruising, so I counted that as a win. Hazel had always been good at explaining away things she didn't want to think too hard about. She had a level of blind eye to the supernatural that she definitely hadn't learned from Aunt Mags.

I turned the screen to show Dante that we'd gotten off scot free, then replied to her message with an *I love you!* and about six dozen emojis. My guilt in digital form.

My car waited in the airport lot where I'd left it in long term parking, and I paid an astronomical fee to retrieve it. The drive to Shadow Hollow took no time at all, since my foot was to the floorboard and my mind was already in Christina's basement, where we might *finally* find answers.

Christina must have heard our car doors slamming shut - either that, or she harbored some serious psychic powers—because she opened the door as we walked up her front porch steps an hour later.

"Good. You made it," she stated ominously, stepping back to let us into her house. She looked as posh as she usually did with her long black hair in an elegant chignon at the nape of her neck and a white wrap-front blouse over chic skinny jeans.

Next to Christina, I felt downright hideous sometimes. But I couldn't even be mad at her, because her loyalty as a friend was second to none.

"I have everything set up in the basement," she told me as she closed the door behind us. "Do you guys need to freshen up? Can I offer you food or drink?"

I glanced at Dante, then said, "I'm okay for now. I just want to get this over with."

He nodded, albeit reluctantly. I'd heard his stomach gurgle on the drive over. His willingness to ignore his hunger pains in lieu of what I wanted made my insides tingle. Was this a relationship? *Weird.*

We marched downstairs, where we set about casting the circle, calling the quarters, and preparing the sacred space for our working. In a perfect world, we would have all taken sacred baths, anointed ourselves, and meditated to clear our minds and center before the spellcasting. But when was the world *ever* perfect? Christina might have taken the time for that shit before we arrived, but my patience for it waned the longer I'd gone without my powers. And if I knew Dante at all, he scoffed at the ceremonial stuff.

Christina had moved everything off the altar except for a white pillar candle and a map of the United States that dominated the table. The three of us posted up around the table—Dante and me on one side, Christina facing us from the other side.

"The blood?" she asked, looking pointedly at me.

"Oh. Yeah." I undid the clasp on the necklace and held it out by the chain, letting the vial fall into her offered palm.

She did a quick anointment over the vial: dunked in salt, smudged in sage, spritzed with water, and passed through the flame of the pillar candle. Then she uncapped it and held it over the map.

She upended the Victorian vial over the middle of the Atlantic Ocean, and a stream of Hazel's blood flowed viscously onto the map's surface. Instead of being immediately absorbed by the paper, the blood quivered and turned into a dark red pearl that rested like a shiny marble atop the sheet.

Christina held both hands over the map, and a brisk wind rose in the basement—the manifestation of her true power as an air witch. She held it back during coven meetings so that she didn't break anyone's concentration or blow out our ritual candles, so it was nice to see her let loose. Nice for her, too, it appeared, as she closed her eyes and her face settled into a kind of ecstasy.

I knew that feeling. I missed that feeling. When you hadn't used your power in a couple days, and you finally did it was like taking a bra off in mid-August.

"Dante, take my hands," she murmured, turning her palms over.

He obeyed, their palms locking together. I thought I felt a low-level hum coming from him. The manifestation of his power, maybe, but I could have been imagining it. Spirit witches didn't manifest with an element that a non-witch could feel or sense. Watching them hold hands as Christina began the incantation reminded me of everything I'd lost.

I'd never be able to cast with Dante. I felt irrationally angry, and a little jealous, to boot.

"Blood like water flows, water like life goes," Christina intoned. "Blood to water, water to blood."

The incantation seemed... Well, anticlimactic. It definitely didn't have the same panache as the Latin Dante had used during our last spell. But the words were never the catalyst. The words used simply gave a witch focus so that the intent could shine through.

For several long moments, Christina and Dante chanted the phrase as Christina's air power raced through the room. I watched the map intently, my heart thudding sluggishly, trying to race because it knew that it should in that moment. Damn undead blood.

Then the little pearl of blood began to move, and the chant trailed off into watchful silence. The blood bead rolled towards the shape of the US, barreling over the east coast, through North Carolina, Tennessee, Kentucky, Missouri... all the way to Montana.

I gaped at the bead as it halted unnaturally on the page. "What now?"

"I was prepared for any option." Christina knelt down beneath the altar table and dug around for a few seconds before emerging with another accordion-folded map. She unfolded the paper and spread it out over the map of the world, then reached for the vial with Hazel's blood.

"A map of Montana," I said, raising an eyebrow. "Do you have a map of *every* state under there?"

Christina grinned as she uncapped the vial. "In my defense, my father was a truck driver for forty years. I already had them. And I *assumed* we were looking for a lake here in the U.S. If the blood had gone to Senegal, we'd be in trouble."

I stared down at the map with shivers coursing up my spine. "Weird that it went to Montana."

"Could be a coincidence," Christina assured me.

We repeated the ritual—pouring the blood onto the map, then Christina and Dante sharing power by holding hands and chanting. The blood became a red marble again, and when the energy was right, it rolled into place.

Right into the middle of the Crazy Mountains outside town.

The bead fell apart and sank into the paper, forming a roughly oval shape between a cradle of the topographic mountains. Nearby, a little golden dot labeled *Shadow Hollow* was etched into the map like a brand.

Christina looked up at me, her eyes wide. "I think it's safe to say it isn't a coincidence that you ended up here, Will. In fact, I think maybe fate made sure you did."

FOURTEEN

I paced Christina's kitchen from doorway to the expensive stainless steel fridge that could house two, maybe three dead bodies, quivering with nervous energy.

"I don't believe in fate," I said for the fourth time, shooting a glance at Christina and Dante. I hated the way my hands were shaking, but I was totally wigged out from the ritual. From finding out that everything we'd been searching for had led us right here. Right back to Shadow Hollow.

Dante was bent over a plate of leftovers from the Bloode ritual—cold buffalo wings, potato salad, and a hamburger bun piled high with lunchmeat and so much mustard it oozed out the edges. He looked at me over his messy sandwich, arching one brow. "Why are you glaring at me? I'm not in charge of fate."

Christina held a delicate wine glass perched between her forefinger and middle finger as she watched me pace. "Willow, you cannot be a witch and also not recognize the serendipity of life on this planet. Someone is moving our chess pieces every day."

"Yeah, sure, *we* are." I turned on my heel at the fridge and headed back towards the door. Christina's house was so new, the floorboards didn't even creak. After living in my Aunt Mags' hundred-year-old farmhouse for a decade, where the floors sang like an orchestra, Christina's floors felt like sorcery. "*We* manipulate our chess boards. Not a deity or the universe or three old ladies weaving the threads of fate or some shit."

Dante snorted and reached for a wing. "She has such a way with words, doesn't she?"

Christina ignored him. "Magic changes things, Will. It adds a new level of universal control that we have no part in."

I shook my head. "No. I make my own decisions."

"Sure, but what drives your decisions?" Christina asked patiently. "It's not just your own wants and needs. It's outside forces. It's something whispering in your ear. What drew you to Shadow Hollow in the first place?"

I sank onto a stool at the center island and sighed. "I followed Corwin here. He moved here because he heard it was a safe place for magicals."

"And it is," Christina agreed with a sage nod. "But something drove him here. Something put the idea in his head. And something made it so that you two became friends before he ever even heard the words *Shadow Hollow*."

I couldn't begin to wrap my head around that kind of cosmic game board. Chess pieces played out by unseen hands, everything connected, everything with a reason and a purpose. It seemed like too much—too many threads to keep up, too many turns that could be made, too much that could go wrong. Way too complicated to be real.

But it *was* weird that I ended up in Shadow Hollow only to find out—later—that a Goode witch would find the lake and undo the curse.

Lacking the brain energy to formulate any other response, I said, "But I'm not a Goode witch anymore, so it can't be me."

Christina inclined her head, waving her wine glass. "Sure. Minor setback when you got sick and decided to survive the best way you knew how. But you aren't the only Goode witch. Maybe you're the catalyst to get your sister here. The same as Corwin was the catalyst to get *you* here."

I scoffed. "That would never happen. I don't think Hazel's ever left Georgia."

"That doesn't mean she won't," Christina pointed out. "Especially if it was for you."

Dante tossed back the last of his beer and reached for a new can as he spoke up. "Ignoring the idea of fate or coincidence, because we could argue about this for days, what do we do now? Do we go to the lake?"

I sighed again—a long, loud, irritated sound. "Yeah. I think we do."

WE PILED into Christina's SUV—me riding shotgun, Dante in the back—and used the blood-stained map as our guide.

Where the blood had settled into the porous paper and dried, it had taken on the look of a rust-colored lake. But beneath the blood, the map hadn't indicated any body of water at all. Just a valley formed between a circular ridge of mountains in the Crazies. No blue blob, no lake name, nothing but green topography. Which meant we would be walking into the mountains blind.

I wasn't an outdoorsy type. My adventures usually involved big cities, bar hopping, and experiencing life as a local, not a tourist. My only experience in the "wild" was when I toured the African savannah from the back of an air conditioned safari Jeep. So imagine my surprise when we rolled into a parking lot marked Crazy Mountain Forest Park, and a mass of winding trails disappeared into the trees ahead of us.

"I'm not dressed for hiking," I said. "These shoes cost way too much. I'll stay here."

Christina rolled her eyes, twisting the key out of the ignition. "It's not an intense hike. They have an easy trail meant for beginners. We go up, we look down into the valley, we see if there's a lake. Easy."

"Does not sound easy," I grumbled but took off my seatbelt anyway.

The sun shone bright from a clear, cloudless sky, but the air had a chill of autumn to it that made me glad I'd pilfered one of Christina's leather jackets from her hall closet. I tied the sash to keep the two sides closed around me and fell into step between my two friends as we took the trail marked with a giant green circle.

We chatted for a while about what we'd figured out, what we knew, how it all might roll together, but after about twenty minutes, we were all too out of breath to continue carrying on a conversation. I apparently wasn't the only member of our misfit party that didn't have the lungs and legs for hiking.

It took nearly an hour to reach the summit of the hiking path. We left the trees behind for a ridge overlooking a magnificent view—a bowl formed by craggy, snow-capped mountains. The valley was filled with green pine trees that looked abnormally bright beneath the sunlight.

"Is this it?" I asked Christina, who'd carried the map on our journey upwards.

She shrugged. "Don't know. I don't see any water."

All I saw beneath us was a sea of pointed pine trees, so I had to agree with her. Had we come all this way for nothing?

"Down?" Dante asked.

"No," I said firmly, as Christina nodded and said, "I think so."

Odds were against me, two to one.

So, we descended.

We didn't talk for a long time as we navigated the treacherous journey downhill. It wasn't terribly steep here, but the ground was loose and crumbly, which made for a dangerous trek. I lost my balance more than once, only to be saved at the last damn minute by Dante's steady hands.

But finally, we made it to the base of the mountain and ventured into the forest.

The sunlight disappeared immediately, as the trees were densely packed with a thick canopy overhead. Christina, always prepared, pulled a flashlight from her backpack and shone the arc of light ahead of us so that we could see where we were stepping.

At some point, I managed to pull ahead of both of them. All three of us were watching the forest intently for threats or wildlife, but none of us were looking for magical barriers.

Not until I slammed right into a squishy wall and fell backwards like a domino.

"Will!" Dante dropped to his knees beside me, his

hands hovering over me. "What happened? Where are you hurt?"

I shoved his hands away and sat up, my head still spinning but only minutely. "I'm fine. Stop it. There's something here."

Christina stepped past us and reached out, walking forward until her hand hit the same barrier that had knocked me down. "It's a magical barrier. A wall to keep people out."

Dante helped me to my feet and I dusted off the ass of my jeans before walking up to the wall and pressing my palm against it. I walked down the barrier, trailing my fingers against the strange, jelly-like substance, searching for any chinks in the armor.

"It's old," Dante remarked. He had both hands pressed against the barrier, eyes screwed shut. "Thirty years. Maybe more."

"So someone set this barrier and left it," Christina mused. She touched her fingers to the wall and a strong wind danced through the trees, making the branches on the trees clack all around us like a discordant symphony. "It doesn't respond to my magic at all."

"Yeah, mine either," Dante agreed, letting his arms drop. "So how do we get through?"

"Only a Goode witch can find the lake," I parroted. I grasped the vial around my neck and held it out. "Hazel's blood."

Without waiting for them to throw their two cents

in, I opened the vial and dipped my fingers in one at a time, wetting the tips with Hazel's blood. It was a hunch based on the whole "only a Goode witch can find the lake" thing, and I was going to feel really fucking dumb when it didn't work.

But the moment Hazel's blood touched the barrier, a flash of light burst from the magic, blinding me. I threw up an arm a moment too late. When the light faded, I was left with the burn of afterimage on my vision, and stood blinking for several long moments before I could see again.

"What the hell was that?" Dante grunted.

"Magic," Christina replied dryly.

I finally managed to see past the white spots in my vision. Shock rippled through me.

I could see the barrier.

Sizzles of fire magic like embers raced across the wall. I reached out again, this time bracing myself for the flash of light, but it didn't happen. My hand passed through the barrier with a strange, suction feeling, and I took a tentative step forward until my face and torso passed through.

Then I was on the other side.

More pine trees stretched around me, but instead of dark, shadowy spaces between them, I could see the glint of sunlight on water, and I could smell the wet, green scent of moss and lakewater.

"It worked!" I turned to face Christina and Dante, only to find they weren't there. The barrier wall showed nothing but dark pine forest as far as I could see.

But when I passed back through the wall, they were right where I'd left them. Not just a barrier then, but a glamour, too. To hide the lake from prying eyes.

"What'd you see?" Christina asked, her face alight with interest.

"The lake is there. Just beyond the trees. Here," I said, uncapping the vial and holding it out for them. "Dip your fingers in. I think Hazel's blood is the key to passing through the barrier."

Christina made a face, but stuck her fingers into the vial one by one until she dripped with Hazel's blood, then stepped aside so that Dante could do the same. I closed the vial then let it fall against my chest, before pressing my still-bloody fingers against the barrier and sluicing back through the magic.

Only... neither of them followed me.

I poked my head back through to find them both slamming their bloodied hands against the wall.

"It's not working," Dante huffed.

"Why?"

"My guess? Because we aren't Goodes," he replied with a shrug. "It's Hazel's blood, but we aren't *her* blood."

Christina gasped. "You're right. We can't use her blood. It doesn't belong to us in any way."

"So I have to go alone?" I shivered. My body was still on the lake side, and it was as if the lake were watching me, eyes on my back. "I don't know if I can…"

Dante stepped up to me and leaned to press his lips to mine. The kiss was much more PG-13 than most of the liplocks we shared, though to be fair, it was hard to steer towards R-rating territory when my tits and ass were on the other side of a magical barrier.

But I drew strength from his kiss, and I had a feeling that was exactly what he intended for me to do.

"You can do this," he said. "Go."

So I tugged my head back through the barrier.

The silence on this side was broken only by birdsong and the lap of water. I angled towards the glint I could see between the thinning trees, jamming my shaking hands into the pockets of Christina's coat so I didn't have to see them shake.

I broke from the trees into brilliant sunlight on the rocky shore of a huge lake. I gaped at the tableau, shocked to see the open sky and the sunlight glinting off the surface of the water like a million tiny diamonds. This was *not* visible from overhead on the ridge. The magic protecting this place was incredible.

Something told me to dip my bloody fingers in the water. So, I sidled right up to the edge, kneeled on the smooth, colorful stones, and leaned over, washing Hazel's blood off in the tiny lapping waves.

I sat for a long time, unmoving, while nothing happened. The surface of the lake spread like a smooth jewel, and the only visible motion was the occasional bird darting in and out of the trees surrounding the lake.

Until a head appeared from the water.

She emerged in increments—first her turquoise hair, then her pale forehead, her vivid, cerulean eyes burning like blue coals. Then her shoulders, clad in a gray cloak over an old fashioned white dress, shapely curves, wide hips, until she stood right before me, only her feet and ankles submerged.

And not a single inch of her was wet.

I tilted my head back to look up at her, too stunned to move. In return, she eyed me warily.

The woman's enigmatic face didn't change as she said, "You are not the Goode witch."

"No," I hedged, "but I was a Goode witch. Before—"

"Before you sacrificed your powers for life. I know. I know all." The woman stepped forward, water splashing around her ankles as she reached towards my neck.

I stumbled away from her, startled by the sudden closeness of her, but my legs got tangled beneath me and I fell flat on my ass in the rocks.

She chuckled mirthlessly. "Scared little guppy." She reached out and wrapped her fingers around the vial that held Hazel's blood - what was left of it, anyway. She jerked the vial against the chain, snapping it off my neck. "She's in here. I can sense her."

Uncapping the vial, the water woman waved the vial beneath her nose and nodded. "Yes. Her blood, but not her. You're a clever vampire. Blood is potent. Like water, it holds the key to life, to memory, to magic." Her thumb pressed against the cap, sealing the vial once more, and she slipped it into her dress pocket. "I'll be keeping this."

"That's mine!"

"You stole the necklace from an honest trader in a Moroccan market," the woman said, her voice unwavering. "And you stole the blood from the Goode witch it belongs to. So, no, my dear, neither is yours by the laws of the universe."

I crossed my arms over my chest, going for haughty but probably looking ridiculous, since I was still sprawled on the rocks. "How did you know that?"

"I told you. I know all." She turned around and began to wade back into the water.

"Hey, wait!" I scrambled to my feet and splashed into the shallows after her.

She whirled around, raising one eyebrow as she stared at my legs submerged in the lake. "The audacity of you, child. You were not invited."

"Please," I pleaded. "You're my only hope in finding answers. Someone's placed a curse on all vampires, and we think there's a possibility this curse could bring about the end of the world. We need to know who and why and how to beat it. Everything we've discovered led us to you."

The woman lifted her pointed nose in the air and looked down it at me. "Bring the Goode witch to me," she said imperiously. "She is our only hope."

Then she burst like a geyser, a waterfall roaring back towards the water, and was gone.

FIFTEEN

We were a subdued party as we passed through the door to Aubrey's that evening.

My expensive boots were still covered in dirt and grime from our walk in the woods, and Christina's chignon had long since been replaced by a more serviceable ponytail. We were hot, crusted with dried sweat, and I was ready to eat the diner out of house and home. I didn't *need* to eat people food, but my tendency to eat my feelings in life followed me in undeath.

George Summers, the proprietor, waved at us from the register and motioned that we should choose whatever table we'd like. He was a big, broad-shouldered man in his early sixties with a long salt-and-pepper braid and dark bronze skin. I'd heard that his wife had died recently, and he looked it. He hadn't shaved in a while, so his scruffy beard matched his hair, and his plaid shirt—usually pressed and tucked into his dark jeans—was rumpled and loose around his waist.

We chose a booth near the door, where Evie, the little pixie blonde waitress, took our orders. In the silence after she left, the three of us stared at one another. I had a feeling none of us knew where to start.

Luckily, we were saved from trying to gather our thoughts as George came to say hello.

"Christina," he said, putting a friendly hand on her shoulder. "How's your mother?"

"As ornery as ever," Christina replied. George and Christina's mother had known one another when they lived on the Res together, long before Christina's birth. She laid her hand over his and leveled an empathetic gaze on him. "But how are *you*?"

George wasn't a man of emotion. He let his hand fall away from her shoulder and shrugged noncommittally. "I'll survive. Willow, nice to see you."

I nodded, then motioned to Dante. "This is my friend, Dante."

"Boyfriend," Dante corrected with a grin, offering George his hand.

I flushed hot from head to toe and agreed. "Boyfriend."

George's smile turned wistful, and he shook

Dante's hand. "This one's trouble, boy. Good luck. Hold her close."

"Hey!" I protested, but we all laughed anyway. He wasn't wrong.

As George walked away, Evie returned to fill our coffee cups, even though we'd barely taken a few sips. Once she'd topped us off and pranced to the next table, I sighed.

"We need to talk about it," I said glumly.

"There's nothing to talk about," Dante replied. "We're back at square one. We have no answers. No means of finding answers."

But Christina shook her head and looked pointedly at me. "That's not exactly true."

I raised an eyebrow. "What do you mean?"

"Hazel."

I shook my head so hard my undead brains rattled. "Nope. No way. We aren't ripping her out of the comfortable life she's made."

"You heard the lake witch," Christina reminded me gently. "Hazel's our only hope."

"Then let the world burn," I snapped. I lifted my coffee to my lips and drank deeply so that I didn't have to say anything else.

Hazel was everything good and wholesome in my world. Our lives had been torn to pieces not once, but twice. First, when our parents died and we had to go live with Aunt Mags. Then second, when Aunt Mags died suddenly. At eighteen, Hazel became my guardian, and that wasn't fair to her. But she did her best to provide for me all through the four years before I graduated high school. She had to sell off Aunt Mags' beautiful farmhouse and work overtime to pay for our tiny little garage room at a friend's house.

Then I'd turned seventeen and taken off for parts unknown, and maybe I'd torn her life to pieces, then. A third time. Leaving her all alone with all our memories.

But the life she'd built since then was a good one. A good job. A comfortable, clean home she didn't have to work overtime to keep. I couldn't uproot her again. I couldn't do that to her.

I loved her too much. I loved her more than I loved the world.

Dante leaned forward on his elbows, his face grave. "If you don't involve her, she'll be another casualty in whatever's coming."

Fear danced along my spine, and I gripped my coffee mug tighter. "I'll think about it."

The tension at the table was thick enough to choke. Even Evie was staying far, far away for the moment. I drank more of my coffee and avoided looking at either of my friends.

Christina was the first to give and finally cleared the air. "So, I'm thinking about opening a tea shop."

I set my mug down with a clunk and blinked. "A tea shop?"

"You know, like a Starbucks except *only* tea. Iced

tea, hot tea, maybe pastries to go with it. And get this," she added, a bit of excitement creeping into her voice, "I'd sell herbs out of the backroom. Like a secret occult herb shop. Alice doesn't have a big selection at Mystique, so it's not like I'd be competing with her."

"I like it," I said. "I think you should go for it. You've got your dad's inheritance, right? Spend it on your startup."

"That's the plan. You really think I could make it work here? In Shadow Hollow?"

"Well, George's coffee is a bit like drinking diesel fuel, and there are a lot of women in this town who would probably appreciate a better option. So, yeah."

We exchanged smiles, and the tension that had been swirling menacingly around us evaporated. My heart ached for Sarah and the friendship I'd lost, but at least I still had Christina.

And I still had Corwin, whenever he decided to rejoin the world of the living.

As if conjured by Christina's single mention of her name, Alice came through the front door of Aubrey's on a background of jangling cowbell. She greeted George with a grin and a hug, and they exchanged a few words before he pointed at our table.

Alice looked around to follow his gesture, and her grin widened. "Willow! Christina!"

George turned away to his kitchen window, and Alice gripped the strap of her giant canvas purse in one hand as she weaved through the occupied tables to us.

"Fancy seeing you here!" she said, leaning to kiss Christina's cheek, and then mine. She looked earthy today, with her long brown hair hanging free around her thin shoulders and comfy sandals on under her patchwork maxi-dress. "I'm just picking up some dinner to take back to the store. I need to place an order tonight, which means staying late and doing inventory." She made a face and gave a kind of half-hearted shrug that made her look a bird stretching its wings. "Will, you should stop by for a reading after you eat!"

"I don't know," I hedged, glancing at Christina. "I'm in the middle of a drama."

"The middle of a drama is the best time to *have* a Tarot reading," Alice insisted. "I won't take no for an answer, and you know it. Drop by. Bring the tall, dark, and hunk-some." She winked at Dante. "Catch you later!"

As she flitted back towards the register to retrieve her plastic bag of food and pay, Christina smiled and shook her head. "The woman's always operating with the same speed of a hummingbird's wings."

"How'd you get out of having to go for a reading?" I griped.

Christina chuckled. "Because she forced me into it last weekend."

Evie arrived with our plates, and I sighed dramatically. "Alice's readings are going to be the death of me."

THE LIGHTS WERE ALREADY out at Mystique by the time Dante and I scraped dust off our shoes on the welcome mat, but Alice had left the door unlocked for us. *Of course* she did, because she knew I wouldn't say no to her demands.

Mystique was barely two years old and was the only occult store in Shadow Hollow. It had been a rough couple years for Alice getting it off the ground. But Alice was nothing if not optimistic, and she pulled through the roughest patch of it with steel grit and daring that I found inspiring, if not downright fucking terrifying. More than anyone, Alice taught me to never underestimate a woman in a dress with magic on her side.

I pushed open the glass door, and the delicate tinkle of windchimes announced our presence. A single recessed spotlight illuminated the empty space at the front of the store, where Alice had placed comfy armchairs for lounging atop a plush area rug in midnight blue. The only other light came from the open doorway behind the register that led to the storeroom.

Alice appeared in this doorway and her face lit up. "Yay, you're here! Give me two seconds. I'll meet you in the reading room."

I left Dante browsing in the spellbook aisle and obediently crossed to the back left corner of the store, where Alice had raised a mixture of curtains and tapestries to form a kind of "room" that housed her card reading table.

I swept aside a green-and-black tapestry depicting the tree of life in a Celtic style and stepped into the dim space beyond, squinting against the gloom.

Alice had left a thick, glass-encased candle burning, and the smell of sage permeated the air. The candle couldn't dispel all the shadows in the tiny corner space, but it cast enough of a glow on the card table for me to see Alice's Tarot cards waiting in their black velvet bag.

I took a seat, tucking my legs beneath the gauzy, layered scarves covering the table, and I'd no sooner gotten comfortable, than Alice slipped through the opening in the curtains.

"So," she said cheerfully as she plopped into her chair. "Drama, huh?"

"Big time," I agreed glumly. "Think you can get me some answers?"

"I'm sure gonna try." She slipped her deck out of the velvet bag and began to shuffle, her gaze on me instead of the cards. "Can you tell me anything about it?"

"It's... family stuff," I said, which wasn't a lie. *Only a Goode witch*, etcetera. I already felt terrible having dragged Christina into this mess. At least one of my friends could remain fancy-free about the curse and the end of the world.

Alice nodded sagely. "Ah. Family stuff can be pretty harsh. I get it. Well, I won't force you to talk about it, but if you ever need to, you know where to find me."

"Thanks, Alice," I said, and meant it.

"All right!" she crowed happily. "Let's see what the cards have in store for you tonight."

She began dealing out on the table, placing five cards in a distinct pattern before she passed the whole deck to me. "Keep dealing. Follow the pattern until you run out of cards."

I accepted the deck, surprised by the weight of them in my hands. Alice didn't read with any puny playing cards - these were the real deal: tall, thick, heavy cardstock with brilliant artwork for both the front and back of each.

I followed her lead, dealing one card at a time to each of the five piles she'd made. Halfway through the thick pile, my hands grew warm and tingly. Alice may not have been a blood-born witch like me or Christina, but she had a special power all her own. The cards did, too, I thought.

Finally, I ran out of cards.

Alice nodded, her gaze raking over the five haphazard piles. She reached out and turned over the final card for the pile closest to her.

"Eight of Cups," she murmured, sliding her finger over a stack of golden cups in the foreground that looked like it was missing a piece. "Disenchantment.

You're lacking emotional fulfillment. Something's holding you back from feeling whole."

My mind immediately snapped to my loss of powers, and how raw that loss had felt this week. "That's true."

Alice nodded. "I know." She flipped over the next card. "Three of Wands. Opportunity. Clarity on the challenges you have ahead."

"I definitely *do not* have clarity," I griped, slouching lower in my seat.

"You will." Alice's tone was so assured, I almost believed her. She turned over the third card.

The change happened swiftly. Alice's fingers paused over the card for only a second, and then she stiffened, her whole body going ramrod straight and still as stone. Her brown gaze lifted to me, and it was like two white veils fell over her eyes, removing all color.

She grabbed the table with both hands, so violently one pile of cards tipped sideways and spilled off the surface. She didn't acknowledge it. "Willow Goode. You must leave Shadow Hollow."

My heart did a little skip and gave a few dying gurgles as terror and adrenaline pumped through my sluggish veins. "Alice, what's going on?"

"Shadow Hollow is no longer the safehaven it once was for your kind," Alice went on, ignoring my question. Her voice even sounded different, like something deeper and darker was layered over her usual tone.

I scooted my chair back but didn't take my eyes off her. "Alice, is that you?"

She inclined her head, and her long brown hair cascaded over her chest. "A version."

I gulped. What the fuck did *that* mean?

"I don't want to leave Shadow Hollow," I told her. "It's my home."

"Home or not," a version of Alice said, "Shadow Hollow will be the last thing you ever know. If you do not leave, you will die here."

SIXTEEN

Immediately after delivering news of my imminent death, the white film over Alice's dark eyes faded, and she blinked at me, surprised. "Oh! Did I knock the cards down? Darn. I'm so clumsy."

She leaned over and started gathering cards, humming to herself.

"What the hell was that?" I demanded, still gripping the edge of my chair like it was the only thing holding me to reality.

Alice straightened, her thick eyebrows drawing together. "What was what? I'm sorry I knocked them off. It's not a normal day if I'm not knocking things over. I come by it honestly. My mother was horrendously clumsy."

Did she not... remember? She sat *right there* across from me and said those things. Did I hallucinate it?

"Alice," I said, "you told me if I stayed in Shadow Hollow, I'd die."

She stared at me, her palm still resting on the stack of cards she'd retrieved from the concrete. "I did... what?"

"You don't remember?"

Shaking her head slowly, she said, "I read the Eight of Cups. The Three of Wands. But when I turned over the third card, I knocked the pile..." Her voice trailed off as she glanced over the edge of the table, as if she couldn't quite piece together reality in her brain.

"No," I said shortly, not because I was angry with her, but because I was thoroughly freaked the fuck out. "You read two cards, and then some weird thing happened, like you were abducted by aliens, and you told me if I stayed in Shadow Hollow, I would die!"

"I did no such thing!" Alice replied, looking horrified at the thought.

"You did," I said. "Is there a history of prophecy in your family? Was there a blood-born witch in your ancestry?"

Alice shrugged helplessly. "I—I don't know. I just like to read cards."

"And make prophecies, too," I said, fear finally becoming a full-fledged monster inside me. I reached down to grab my purse off the floor.

"Where are you going?"

"Home. To pack my bags and buy a plane ticket." I stood, tossing the strap over my shoulder and looked down at her, softening. "You should hone that, you know. Figure out who the blood-born witch was in your family, see if she's still alive. We live much longer than humans, so she's probably still around. She could help you get control of those visions."

I leaned over and popped a kiss on her hairline, then sprinted from the store like the devil was on my heels.

For all I knew... he was.

I WAS *DONE*.

Done trying to find answers from a trail of unrelated breadcrumbs. Done trying to save the world, when the world hadn't done shit to save me. If all I got out of this week was a committed relationship and an extended vacation somewhere else, then that was fine by me.

In the car on the way to Sarah's, I told Dante what had happened during the reading. He scoffed at me taking "the little wiccan chick's" prophecy as truth, but he hadn't been there. He hadn't seen the way her body changed—lengthened, hardened, like someone else had slipped into her skin. He hadn't seen her pure white eyes or heard that strange double voice.

Alice's prophecy was the one thing in this hellish week that felt like an answer.

The answer: *Get the fuck out!*

I'd stayed in Shadow Hollow way too long this go 'round. The universe was giving me the kick in the pants I needed to leave, and I wasn't going to ignore it.

Plus, what did I have to stay for? I wasn't the Goode witch. I didn't have the power, and I didn't have the balls to drag Hazel out of her life. Not for this.

No, I was just a Goode vampire, and I definitely wasn't going to save the world by sucking on the necks of everyone I met.

I'd accumulated more crap than usual in the last six months of being here. Usually, I could pack and go in a matter of minutes, but I ended up having to load down a couple of new boxes, and then jam eight of them in my car. While Dante made a circuit in the house unplugging things and making sure it was ready to sit fallow, I coaxed Castor and Pollux into their carriers with treats, packed up their toys, food, and bowls, and added them to the chaos in my backseat.

Then we locked up Sarah's cottage and headed for Corwin's house.

I'd called him the moment I left Mystique and caught him up to speed—including the prophecy stating that Shadow Hollow wasn't safe for vampires. But no matter how I tried to convince him, Corwin refused to leave. He'd just wearily told me, "Do what feels right, Willow."

A fat lot of help, he was.

I turned into Corwin's neighborhood, still grieving for my life at Sarah's. For the life she and I had made together, the fun we'd had, the late nights and the shopping trips and the ritual magic. She'd been the closest thing to a sister I'd had since leaving Hazel alone in Georgia.

Corwin's neighborhood was one of the oldest in town with the quirkiest set of residents. The big white house at the front of the neighborhood was a notorious bachelor pad usually filled with college students that liked to party. If the football-stadium shine from the backyard was any indication, they were already throwing down. Across the street from them was the old Halliwell place, a notoriously haunted house that had set empty for years. The dark windows of the place looked like empty eyes that watched us as we passed.

Corwin's big blue Queen Anne sat near the back of the cul-de-sac, a single lamp glowing orange in a downstairs window. Dante grabbed the first of the boxes, while I lugged Castor and Pollux up the drive to the front door.

Corwin answered on the second doorbell ring. I hardly recognized him—his brownish-blond beard had taken over his usually clean-shaven face, and his hair was lank and unwashed. His T-shirt was stained and rumpled over his sweats. He looked sallow in the porch light, with deep circles beneath his eyes making him resemble more a skeleton than a vampire. Both his bloodshot eyes and the intense wave of sickly-sweet gin coming from his person told me he was more than a few sheets to the wind.

"Dear gods," I said. "You look like shit."

Corwin glared at me but stepped aside and held out a hand. "Release them in the living room."

I kept my gaze on him as I passed into the house. Where the hell was the real Corwin? The prim and proper, OCD version I knew and loved? I knew everyone grieved differently, but this was harsh.

In his fancy parlor, I opened the little metal doors on the cats' carriers. They both eased from the interiors, noses sniffing at the air and fur standing on end.

"They'll probably hide for a while," I told Corwin as he came into the room, carrying boxes alongside Dante. "And they're still grieving."

"We'll keep grieving together," Corwin said gruffly. He set his boxes down next to Dante's just inside the door.

"I'll grab the rest," Dante said. "So you can say goodbye."

In his absence, Corwin and I stared at one another over the empty expanse of the living room. Castor and Pollux were slinking around the couch, sniffing the wooden legs and the Oriental rug, their bodies low to the ground. On guard.

He cleared his throat. "So you think Alice's prophecy is true?"

"I don't know what to think, but I don't want to die. Not anymore than I wanted to die last year."

The reminder sent us both back to silence. Somewhere in the house, a clock chimed the hour, and the sound was haunting. I counted nine gongs while Corwin and I just looked at each other, neither of us speaking. Neither of us moving. Hell, neither of us even pretending to breathe.

The last two vampires in the world, saying goodbye.

"You could come," I said quietly. "Alice would take the cats."

Corwin shook his head. "I'll take my chances here."

"Why?"

He grimaced. "This is where I loved her. Where I thought I would spend the rest of my life with her. I intend to stay."

I nodded. It made sense, even if I thought he was being dumb. "What if something happens? She said vampires aren't safe here."

Shrugging, Corwin said, "I'll call you if it happens. Keep in touch?"

"Always."

He crossed to me with long strides and wrapped me in his strong, steady arms. I squeezed back, wishing I could take away his pain. Wishing he'd come with me.

Dante returned, setting the last of the boxes atop the pile. "That's everything."

I released Corwin. "Thanks for keeping my things."

"My home will always be here for you," he said.

We shared one more look that said the things neither of us could bring ourselves to speak. *I love you, old friend. Be well. Be safe. Don't die.*

Then I walked out his front door, unsure when—or if—I'd ever see him again.

WE WERE over the Atlantic Ocean sometime in the middle of the night when Dante shook me awake.

I blinked into the low light of the cabin. Most everyone was asleep, with only a few overhead lights on here or there. Beyond the rustle of blankets and light snores, there was only the constant, steady thrum of the plane's engine beneath us.

I sat up and rubbed away the sleep in my eyes before fixing my gaze on my boyfriend. "What? What's wrong?"

"Will," Dante said, his voice low so that only I could hear him. "What happens if Alice's prophecy comes true? You've promised your soul to a demon."

"What?" I shook my head and brushed my hair back from my face. "Dante, you woke me up for this?"

"Hey." He took my hand and pressed it against his

lips. "Be serious for a minute. You promised your soul to a demon upon death."

"Fat lot of good it did, too," I griped, rubbing my forefinger idly against his cheek. "We're running away from Shadow Hollow no closer to answers about the curse or that stupid lake."

He nodded. "If Alice is right, and your life is in danger, whether it's this week or next month or years from now… What are you going to do to make sure the demon can't take what's due?"

A niggling of fear worked its way up my spine. I didn't fancy an eternity at the beck and call of a fiery demon in the underworld. And Dante was right—I'd made the promise. A magical binding.

The only way to fight magic was with magic.

"Do you have your grimoire in your bag?" I asked him.

Raising an eyebrow, he leaned forward and unzipped his bag, then extracted his ornate, leather-bound spellbook. He deposited it on my knees, where the weight of it seemed unreal, like it held many more pages than met the eye.

I had a feeling it did.

And one of those pages *had* to have a way to anchor my soul to the mortal world.

While Dante settled back against his seat to sleep, I turned on my overhead light, opened the Bloode grimoire, and set to reading.

Time would pass, like it always did. For a vampire,

time meant nothing, and it was easy to forget. To reevaluate. To miss home.

But I'd come to find out Alice was right, after all.

The next time I set foot in Shadow Hollow, it would be the last.

Continue reading the Creatures of the Midwest series with book 1
A Vampire in Disguise by Ava Silvers

ACKNOWLEDGMENTS

To Rebecca, thank you. This book would not be what it is without your unwavering support and your belief in this story from its earliest days. You truly helped bring it to life.

To Christian Bentulan, I am in awe of your talent; thank you for creating a cover that is not just beautiful, but is the perfect face for this novel.

And to the ghosts who haunt my halls—whether you meant to or not, thank you for the late-night whispers of inspiration. You were the most unusual of muses.

About the Author

Ava Silvers is an author who specialises in the genre of Urban Fantasy. Ava's storytelling merges from her own lived experiences and imagination. When not writing she finds joy in exploring forgotten towns and haunted hotels, and seeking inspiration from eerie buildings from the past.